MOUNT ST. HELENS

A Summer Stories Anthology

Edited by Carolyn Lamberson

and

The staff of *The Spokesman-Review*

A note from our sponsor

We're happy to help with creation of this book — a celebration of local writers, a peek into the wonder of the natural world, and a tribute to Spark Central, an organization that ignites passion in all of us.

Published by:
The Spokesman-Review
Spokane, Washington

Mount St. Helens: A Summer Stories Anthology
Copyright 2020 The Spokesman-Review

Illustrations by: Molly Quinn/The Spokesman-Review
Mount St. Helens photo: Christopher Anderson/The Spokesman-Review
    Archive
Cover design: Chris Soprych, The Spokesman-Review
Book design: Russel Davis, www.graydogpress.com

ISBN: 978-1-578-78178-5

Printed in the United States of America

Introduction

The creation of *The Spokesman-Review's* Summer Stories series dates back to the winter of 2013-14, when then-editor Gary Graham forwarded to me an article about the *Minneapolis Star-Tribune's* plans to publish a serialized novel. That would be a cool thing to do, I thought. As I thought about it some more, it seemed that Spokane's literary community was giving me clues on how to proceed. My friend and colleague Shawn Vestal was winning accolades for his debut short story collection, *Godforsaken Idaho*. Jess Walter had followed up his *New York Times* bestselling book *Beautiful Ruins* with his first story collection, *We Live in Water*. And Pie and Whiskey, the night of fun and short fiction held during the Get Lit festival each spring, had quickly become the literary event of the year.

What if, I said to Graham, we asked a bunch of Spokane-area writers to submit short stories, and what if we ran them in the Today section on Sundays during the summer months?

Graham's reply? Do it.

Armed with advice from Vestal, Walter and Sam Ligon, co-founder of Pie and Whiskey, we did it, and in 2014 we debuted Summer Stories with tales centered around "the fair," as that year marked the 40th anniversary of Expo '74.

After Graham retired, Rob Curley became editor of *The Spokesman-Review*. From the moment he arrived, he said how much he loved Summer Stories and how cool it would be to turn it into a book. So, in 2020, a bigger, broader Summer Stories celebrated the 40th anniversary of the Mount St. Helens eruption. I gave the authors three prompts, and suggested they could use one, two or all three. The first dealt with "rumblings," and focused on the spring of 1980 when Mount St. Helens awoke. The second, "apocalypse," centered on the eruption, and the quote by volcanologist David Johnston as he frantically radioed his colleagues with the U.S. Geological Survey: "Vancouver! Vancouver! This is it!" The final option was "aftermath," as rivers clogged, trees fell like dominoes and ash covered everything. We made the series longer – expanding from 10 weeks to 17 weeks – and included writers from beyond the Inland Northwest. Some writers kept Mount St. Helens as a central part of their stories. Others mentioned it in passing. A few never mentioned the volcano or the eruption at all.

Now, thanks to generous support from STCU, *The Spokesman-Review* is thrilled to produce the first Summer Stories anthology in book form. All profits from sales of this book will be donated to Spark Central, the Spokane non-profit that provides creative education and outreach for youth.

Carolyn Lamberson, Senior Editor,
The Spokesman-Review

Contents

MOUNT ST. HELENS

A Summer Stories Anthology

The Thick Darkness

Shawn Vestal

1

It came as Father said it would come, a shroud over the sun, a night in the day, a black pall upon the earthly coffin of the wicked.

2

At the campground, the Forest Service man came and asked for $16. "Don't my taxes already run this place?" Father asked, but the Forest Service man told him it was still $8 a night for each campsite, and our large canvas tent was taking up two of them.

"You could get a motel for $16," Father said.

The Forest Service man listened patiently as Father discussed the failings and offenses of the government. Mother watched from the tent-flap door holding Ruth against her cocked hip. Food crates and the 50-gallon water tank filled one picnic table. David and Jeanine played Bible Go-Fish at the other.

The Forest Service man said, "That all may be true, Mr. Constant, but I still am going to need $16 for the night."

Father paid it.

The following morning, we felt the earth tremble beneath our feet, a thrill and a fright. Father began watching the mountain through his binoculars.

3

We were seven, we Constants. Father and Mother and Joel and Jeanine and David and Ruth and me, Peter, the middle boy.

We prayed, kneeling, in the mornings upon arising. We prayed before eating breakfast around the fire. We prayed over our lunches in the forests where we foraged, and we prayed over dinner, and we prayed together a final time each day, on our knees beside the hushing river, before climbing inside the tent for the night, prayed to be taken in the hands of the Lord and uplifted.

4

Father paid for the first day but not the second or third. The earth shook again in the afternoon of the third day, a brief rumbling underfoot, the pines shaking. Father watched the mountain. Steam vented below the peak on the north side. He showed us through the binoculars. Another time he shouted for us to come and see; a blue gas was flowing upward from the mountain. He said the mountain itself was bulging. Its very shape and nature was changing, and who was it who could change the very shape and nature of the world? That night he read to us from Exodus, read of Moses and the stone tablets written by the finger of the Lord.

When the Forest Service man returned, it wasn't to ask for money. It was to tell us we had to leave. The volcano was going to erupt. The earth shook under our feet even as he told us.

"What if we choose to stay?" Father asked him.

"You can't stay, sir," the Forest Service man said. "You don't have a choice."

5

Father brought us here, to this forest and this river, from Bliss, Idaho, where we had moved from Boise after he quit his job at his brother's machine shop, his brother's wickedness having finally become intolerable. Mother said he was proud, but Father said he knew his value. He said too many men had spent their righteousness in submission. Mother surprised us and said: "Your family going hungry won't be counted for much." Father warned her not to try his patience, and Mother asked how did he dare to call his stubbornness righteousness, and Father threw forth his hand, making a sound that would never leave the household. He spent the rest of the night pleading and apologizing to Mother.

In Bliss, we rented a home with one bedroom and a sloping, linoleum-floored kitchen. Mother taught us at home. Father worked at a dairy in Gooding until he lost that job, and worked at the truck stop in Mountain Home until he lost that job, and worked at the lumber yard in Jerome until the manager asked him to stop listening to preachers on the yard radio and Father quit.

"The world hates a free man," he said.

6

We broke down the tent and loaded the Wagoneer and the trailer. Father drove out of the campground, waving amiably at the Forest Service man as we left, and away from the shadow of the great mountain. Mother sang hymns, and some of us sang along. After winding westward for several miles, Father turned onto a dirt road and doubled back, and we were soon traveling east again, back toward the shadow of the mountain. Father stopped on the roadside and we prayed that the Lord would lead us where we were meant to be, and we drove along narrow logging roads with soft, gravel shoulders until we found a meadow along the Green River where a line of tall, thin firs stood sentry along a grassy bank.

"There is always a choice," Father said, as if to himself, as he parked the Wagoneer.

7

We were scared, mostly. Sometimes we were scared of Father. Sometimes we were scared because we were so unlike everyone else and feared we were in the wrong. Sometimes we were scared the world was ending, and we were not righteous enough to be saved. Scared that we would stand on the burning earth and watch our Mother and Father lifted to the heavens. Mostly we were scared because our days had become so strange compared to those that came before, earth shaking without warning and mountains changing shape before our eyes.

8

Mother taught us how to gather beans from lupins and rinse them in the river to prevent poisoning. She taught us how to find oyster mushrooms on fallen alders, though it wasn't the best time for them yet, and she warned us away from bark mushrooms. Father went out to poach an elk but came back with a creel of dappled trout and gigged frogs. We didn't have a fire. The days were cool and fine. We could smell the grass shoots and new buds of spring on the breeze. If Father thought he heard a car, he rushed us into the tent until he had glassed the valley with his binoculars and made sure no one was coming.

9

The mountain was farther away now, but still Father watched it. The tremors came regularly. The bulge on the slope was growing, he said. You could see it. He said the Lord would protect us.

He read to us from Exodus as we ate the bitter lupin beans. "And all the people saw the thunderings, and the lightnings, and the noise of the trumpet, and the mountain smoking: And when the people saw it, they removed, and stood afar off.

"And they said unto Moses, Speak thou with us, and we will hear: But let not God speak with us, lest we die.

"And Moses said unto the people, Fear not: For God is come to prove you, and that his fear may be before your faces, that ye sin not.

"And the people stood afar off, and Moses drew near unto the thick darkness where God was."

10

When we heard the voice of the Lord at last, Father said, it would not appear as a human voice, speaking words. We could not know, or even imagine, how it would manifest, he said, though if we were righteous, we would recognize it because it would be meant for us. He told us the end of this world might seem like something to fear, and it would indeed be fearsome to behold, but for the righteous, it would be the beginning of a glorious, never-ending new day.

Father tuned in the ham radio and listened to the reports. He pored over the map and looked through the binoculars. Mother approached him repeatedly, speaking in such a low voice that we could not hear her words but could hear Father's answers.

He said, "We will not return there, Mother. We will never do it."

He said, "I believe we are protected here."

He said, "We need not fear the manifestations of the Lord."

11

We had finished breakfast and were cleaning the dishes in the river when it began.

The world blurred and rumbled. Hard enough to knock you sideways. Loud enough to swallow all sound. The alders swished and flapped, and a cutbank on the river crumbled into the water. Father shouted as he looked through his binoculars, but we couldn't make out the words. A growl rose from the mountain, from under us, from all around, as of a giant awakening to anger, as of ancient, malevolent machinery groaning back to life.

An explosive crack came from the mountain, and we could not believe what we seemed to be seeing: the mountain crumbling to pieces and rushing toward us. The trees bent, as if before a great wind, and stones began to skitter past us like smaller creatures fleeing a storm. And then, from the crown, the curling, thick pillar of gray and black.

This realm was disintegrating, preparing to reveal whatever lay behind it.

Father kept the binoculars to his eyes and hollered soundlessly. Mother waved at us to go to the Wagoneer. An ashy flow arrived and moved about our feet, deepening. Mother dragged Ruth and David to the back of the wagon. Joel rushed to grab the water tank and stumbled with it to the wagon as the earth flowed around his ankles. A tree flashed past like a bullet, caroming end over end across the river, and then another skidded past. Jeanine ran to me where I sat, stunned, on the felled log with my pocket knife and stick. She took me by the hand and pulled me toward the Wagoneer.

Mother shouted twice for Father, but he didn't turn. She climbed into the driver's seat and started the engine.

12

Inside, we could hear the earth shifting under us. Shuffling, flowing, rising like a river and flowing toward the valley before us. We coughed in the dimming air, wiped our leaking eyes. Mom put the Wagonner into gear, and the back door opened, and Father leapt in, shouting: We'll be crushed! Mother pressed the gas, and we leapt forward.

She drove, lurching and bouncing, and following the direction in which all things were flowing, but the earthy slurry was rising, a gray river flowing toward the Green River, and soon it seized the wagon and stopped us. She started it again, and continued, but still the ground raced past us, around us, and the engine seized again. Father shouted again: We'll be crushed!

13

Above us rose a black column of smoke. Behind us came the moving earth, the flying, fallen forest, and up ahead, somehow, under a canopy of advancing darkness, was the calm blue of a spring morning. Ruth wailed. Father coughed and coughed, and spat. David panicked, shouted that we had to get out, but he pushed futilely at his door. A tree, riding on the ashy flow, crashed into the back window and spun off, cracking it open. The flowing earth sifted in smelling of fire.

Then we began to move. Just a bit, a tiny shift, but then it happened again, and soon we were taken up by the muddy flow, flocked and nudged on all sides by the fallen forest. We watched the ashen flow enter the river ahead of us, darkening the waters, and all things rose into a one thing, all things came apart and reunited in a restless new alchemy of earth and water and rock and tree, and we rode it as the world dimmed and darkened.

It was so fast.

Father shouted and wept as we went, and Mother was silent and watchful, all of us wondering if this was salvation or mere reprieve, all of us flowing and weeping and coughing and praying. When we came to rest what seemed like hours later – filthy, alive, our battered Wagoneer atop a crash of trees in a world made of ash, watching the helicopter hovering above – we entered our new days of wonderment, the days and then the years of ceaseless wonder, each of us alone in it, each of us alone to answer whether the voice of the Lord was the disaster or the deliverance, or neither, or both.

Shawn Vestal is a columnist for *The Spokesman-Review*. He also is an award-winning fiction writer. His debut story collection, *Godforsaken Idaho* (Little A), won the PEN-Bingham prize for debut works. His first novel, *Daredevils* (Penguin Press), won the Washington State Book Award for fiction. A native of Idaho, Vestal lives in Spokane with his family.

Oscitation

Beth Piatote

If it weren't for my daughter's fever, I might never have talked to Susanna.

But we live in a world of rules, and the rule at preschool was no preschool if your kid has a fever. And that's where it started, this strange set of events: my wife, wrapped in her ruby robe, holding our daughter on her lap and handing me the thermometer. It was a Tuesday. I rinsed the thermometer and fetched the children's Tylenol. I held the baby and pressed a cold cloth to her flushed cheeks while my wife got dressed and poured herself a cup of coffee. She called in at work. Then, because the baby was sick and my wife would stay home, I didn't have to stop at the preschool on the way to the archive, which is how I got there early.

And because I was early, I talked to Susanna.

Susanna was neither a friend nor a stranger. We shared the intimacy of a long wooden table. For weeks, we had sat side-by-side, never speaking. It was a relationship of warm indifference. She never looked up when I arrived late, yet I felt her company every day. I only knew her name from the register and from hearing the archivist call her to retrieve paged items.

Working in an archive suspends the rules of ordinary life. Under normal conditions, I would find it intolerable to sit in a wooden chair folded over documents and writing with a pencil for eight hours a day.

But in the archive, we belonged to other worlds like time travelers who had left ordinary life behind. We were loathe to take breaks. One of our table-mates, Jefferson, carbo-loaded at breakfast so he wouldn't have to stop to eat lunch. The rest of us slipped out to eat sandwiches from our lockers while standing in the hallway.

Each afternoon, I left the archive with a light head and sore back and a file full of notes on unbound paper. Each day, my timeline got fatter and the maps and stories more fleshed out. We were like vultures sinking into carrion, stripping and pecking the personal details of strangers from love letters, court records, documents and diaries right down to the bone. At least, the best of us were like that.

The best of us didn't talk to each other except in the hallway before the archive opened, which is where I was that morning.

"You are early today," Susanna said.

"It's purely by accident," I said.

"You should be more careful," she said.

Susanna had a slight German accent, which I began to hear more often after that. As I said, we barely stepped away from our work long enough to eat a sandwich, but as days progressed we began to take that anxious ritual together. I told her about my research on the Minidoka internment camp in Idaho and that I was reading the papers of a war relocation officer.

She asked me how I became interested in Minidoka.

I told her that when I was a boy, my grandfather said something curious. He said: There used to be that place over there, as big as a city. But it's gone now. You can't find it on a map.

Over time, I realized that he was talking about the camp, at a place called Hunt, not far from where I grew up. When it was operating, it was the eighth-largest city in the state. And then it was gone.

"It's never gone," Susanna said.

That seemed like a German thing to say, and I told her so.

"Americans and Germans are different," I said. "Americans have made an art of forgetting catastrophe. Not so the Germans."

"Yes, from the state perspective we have a policy to remember, to expose everything about the war," she said. "But our grandparents talk in riddles, too."

Susanna was writing a dissertation on the 19th century British poet and clergyman Gerald Manley Hopkins, whose papers were in the archive. She had a modest fellowship, which allowed her to rent a room in a house not far from Gonzaga. She said the cat who lived at the house had six toes. This was the extent of personal information that I knew about Susanna.

One day, while I was reading, she pressed her index finger on my elbow.

"Can you help me?" she whispered.

She pointed at a handwritten diary, at a word floating in smudged ink, making it hard to discern.

I studied it closely, careful not to touch it, then whispered each letter: o-s-c-i-t-a-t-i-o-n. She wrote it on a sheet of paper.

"I don't know this word," she said, more to the paper than to me.

I pointed at the door.

She brought her paper to the hallway, where she read the quotation out loud. "I have never felt anything so touching, so contagious, so overwhelming, as the spectacle at which I was yesterday present," she read. "Some 40 young throats breathing out their very hearts and lungs in loud, ecstatic, volcano-like yawning. The tears rose unbidden to my eyes, and I felt a lump and a yearning in my throat: It is not well in general to speak of one's own spiritual history, but here the glory reflects on others rather than oneself – I, too, had my moments of deep oscitation. O what a wondrous, unspeakable relief is this method of oscitation!"

"It's yawning," I said. "To oscitate is to yawn."

Then, without warning, I yawned.

Then she yawned too, because it happens that way, sometimes, that you feel something coming, and you can't quite control it.

I told her I feared my oscitation was not as ecstatic and volcano-like as one might like, and she assured me it was perfectly adequate and quite fitting to the rules of the archive.

I was mildly disappointed in her assessment. Adequate.

Not many days after that, as we were eating lunch in the hallway, Susanna announced that it was her last day.

"Tomorrow I am going to a funeral, and I return to Aachen on Saturday," she said.

The first item hit me harder than the second. How could Susanna be going to a funeral? Who could she possibly know here?

I asked her who had died.

"I've never actually met her," Susanna said. "But I've been living in her house."

"With the cat?" I asked.

"Yes. You see," Susanna said, "I arranged everything with the owner by telephone. But she called me a few days before I came and told me that she had to go to the hospital for a routine matter. She asked me to feed her cat. She said it would only be a few days."

But the woman's condition worsened with time. Susanna had asked to visit, but the woman insisted that she was getting better, and she didn't want to meet Susanna for the first time looking so ill and not at all herself. In the meantime, a choir that the woman belonged to would meet at the house every Wednesday night to rehearse. And as the woman got sicker, different members of her family came to stay so they could visit her at the hospital. Susanna would come home from the archive some nights and hear the washing machine going. Or see fresh eggs in the refrigerator or hair in the shower drain. She seldom saw the actual people, only evidence of their having passed through.

Then the woman died.

The choir showed up to practice songs for the funeral. The woman's parents came to select clothes for the burial. Susanna sorted the stack of mail.

I realized that when Susanna went to the funeral, she would be seeing the woman for the first time. I asked if I could accompany her. It seemed too strange a thing to do alone, and I imagined that I was her only friend. Perhaps Susanna thought so, too, because she agreed.

The next morning, as I got dressed, I thought the strangest thing I would do that day was go to the funeral of a woman whom I'd never met. But life can surprise you.

I kissed my wife. I took the baby to preschool.

I told myself it was a regular day with only an unusual interlude, yet I felt a twinge as I drove past Boone Avenue, past the archive.

Susanna was waiting in the foyer of the funeral home wearing a navy dress. It struck me I would never have seen her in a dress were it not for this circumstance. I wondered about her other clothes that I'd never seen. Her life suddenly became mysterious to me.

We passed together through the receiving line, the family alternately dabbing their eyes and grasping our hands. A few seemed to know Susanna. It was odd how natural it felt to be there with her.

The woman's name was Corinne. We arrived at the open casket and studied her still, gaunt face. Susanna drew a deep breath, and I lightly placed my hand on the small of her back. She seemed to relax then, and we walked together to the chapel.

After the service, I offered to drive Susanna home. It was barely noon, and the sky was open and calm. We sat for a moment in the car. I felt unsure what to say.

"Do you want to see the cat?" she asked.

Indeed I was curious to see the six-toed cat, although it hadn't been on my mind at that moment. I could see the big, smoky-gray cat sitting in the front window looking out at us.

I followed Susanna into the house. The cat had enormous paws, which suited his overall look as a large cat. He had the appearance of a dark cloud but the personality of a sunbeam. He purred and rubbed his head under my hand.

I asked what would become of him. Susanna said she did not know exactly.

Then, without warning, I moved toward Susanna. Or she moved toward me. I will never know who made the first move. But once it started, it did not stop; it was avalanchelike in its unfolding. We made our way to her room as a single animal, gliding, in my imagination, as ice skaters, but in reality more like an elk freeing a branch from its antlers. I was suffocating in the thought of death, of dust, and grasped after her to save me, to make me feel alive.

The thing was, I didn't quite know where to put my hands. Legs? Hips? Back? I kept moving them around, never really committing to one, like a carwash. What was wrong with me? Perhaps it was the pressure of knowing this would be both the first and last time for us, a singular event that would divide the Before from the After.

I stayed with her for a while afterward. We didn't talk. Why would we? Her bags were packed and parked beside the bedroom door. The cat sat in the hallway and licked his giant paw. Eventually, I took a shower and said goodbye.

The next day, a Saturday, I drove past the house. Susanna was gone; I knew this. The cat, too, was missing from the sill. The house was but a shell, as though none of us had ever been there. The sky beyond was a reliable blue, with clouds of white gauze in the distance, and clusters of calla lilies slanted away from the porch. It seemed easy enough to believe that nothing had happened there. Or that what had happened was only a vent, an escape, a great gasping for breath. I longed for it to be only that: a vent that would release enough pressure to go on, and not a fissure that would soon open wide.

Beth Piatote is the author of the story collection *The Beadworkers: Stories* (Counterpoint 2019). She is an associate professor of Comparative Literature and Native American studies at the University of California, Berkeley, where she specializes in Native American literature, Nez Perce language and literature, indigenous language revitalization and creative writing. She is Nez Perce, enrolled with Confederated Tribes of the Colville Reservation. This story was originally published under the title *Rumblings*.

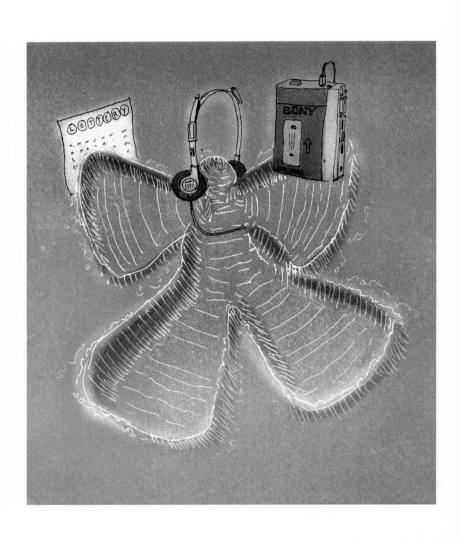

Mayday

Bruce Holbert

College hadn't worked out for Yeller: He had not even learned to drink well. By spring, his second sophomore year at Eastern Washington University – Eastern Washington State College three years before, their mascot, the Savages; little Indians with tomahawks remained in the athletic facility's brick walkway – Yeller was an Eagle and a fairly lost bird.

He opted for college to avoid construction work. It's not that he didn't respect working with your hands: He was no good at it. Upon graduation, most of his high school classmates migrated to the Tri-Cities and employment at the nuclear plant. Ironworkers, boilermakers, machinists, welders, operators: All the union books opened, but Yeller could ruin an anvil with a feather duster. He didn't trust himself on a project that might melt half the state.

Recently, he took work selling knives strong enough to cut metal, out of a briefcase. A customer once inquired why she would want such a knife.

"Don't you think it's better to have a knife that cuts metal and not need it than to need a knife to cut metal and not have it," Yeller responded. He was a sincere person and eager for his clients' comfort. He believed every kitchen ought to be properly equipped.

In the tavern, he chatted up all those he knew: locals and out-of-towners and students – the knives made excellent gifts for parents. Those he didn't, he introduced himself and hunted for the portion of them that bought things. He never felt off duty. It wore him out. One tavern breakfast, he found himself with no one on either stool beside him. Others picked through omelets or stabbed their overeasy eggs with toast, but Yeller no longer noticed the bustle.

The muscles in his shoulders relaxed, and his head lolled a little. It was as calm as he had ever been. He let his breakfast sit. He didn't drink his orange juice. For an entire song, he didn't move. Not the frozen hide-and-seek sort of stillness, but tranquil without effort, like a tree or mountain.

A jukebox song finished, then another. The gears in his head gently engaged. They pressed him someplace poorly lit. He squinted. Light clung to the ground, low and ethereal; it seemed to emit from underneath. Shadows appeared like wraiths, not zombies nor frightening nor silent nor depressed.

Eventually, Yeller recognized he must return to the barstool and his breakfast and his ordinary chaos. He determined he would retain this moment, though. There would be signs. The bartender refilled his coffee. Yeller glanced up. The man wore a simple bill cap, but stitched to its brim was a yellow hoop and inside a silhouetted rodeo rider aboard a rearing horse.

"What time is it?" Yeller asked.

The bartender glanced at his watch. "Half past one."

"What day?"

"Sunday."

The haberdasheries were all closed. Tomorrow, Yeller thought. Tomorrow he would become a cowboy.

Ten minutes later, a drunk woman approached him. Her husband required dialysis, and she wanted to winter him in Arizona. She offered him a lottery ticket for $10.

"I can get my own for half that," Yeller told her.

"But who would it help?" she asked.

He didn't have $10. Breakfast was the end of his cash. He offered her a knife. "It cuts metal," he said.

They traded. "It's sad for me to lose this ticket," she said. "But it may be good luck to you."

Outside, the sun hurt Yeller's eyes. He'd determined today to visit the library. Tomorrow was his midterm in Intro to Biology, a class he hadn't attended in two weeks. He'd encountered a woman in the back row; she'd asked if he knew where to get extra pencils. He offered her his. When the professor began his lecture, she scratched words furiously into her notebook, her pretty face bunched with attention.

She did not notice Yeller wrote nothing, nor did she return the pencil after. The weeks following, Yeller occasionally encountered her on campus. Once his eyes met hers, but Yeller saw nothing like recognition. In fact, her nose wrinkled as if she'd smelled something disagreeable, then she gazed down at her books and hurried past. Thinking of it hurt Yeller's teeth.

On the sidewalk outside, people pointed west at a black line that appeared to be just horizon. Someone with a Walkman radio said a mountain blew up. That mountain, the person said. The one in the news. Yeller continued to the library. There he chose a study carrel on the top floor. The black he thought horizon crept forward. Inside it, beautiful purple lightning fluttered too distant to provide the accompanying thunder. Yeller smelled something like dust. The black cloud climbed the sky, pressing the blue it had not yet erased bluer.

Soon the whole of the sky had surrendered. Outside, streetlights flickered orange light despite it being midday, their luminescence dimmed to dots in the falling ash. Yeller watched a football player he recognized appear, then disappear, then appear again as he made his way to a dorm. Yeller wondered if the man knew he was magic. Not just a witness to a trick but the trick itself.

The library's overhead lights flickered, its indicator for closing. An emergency, an assistant said. She checked out books, though, like business as usual. She didn't know this new sky cut your lungs when you breathed it. She didn't know the Safeway would soon have no food or beer.

No one knew removing the portion over them would require all summer. No one knew it would turn concrete sludge when wet. No one knew Harry Truman was dead or the Toutle River was choked with debris. No one predicted the event would deliver the president. A disaster, the news would call it. It seemed something else to Yeller, and he was now a person with authority, a prophet.

A minor one, yes, not worthy of a chapter in anyone's bible or a cable television show nor a 1-800 number. He patted his chest. The ticket in his pocket remained. He hadn't studied the numbers. They wouldn't be those listed in the paper tomorrow, though, and his name would not appear the next day as a winner. He foresaw this.

Yeller did not forecast surviving two automobile accidents in his own life or suffering an arrest and two nights of jail on a cop's mistake. He didn't see seven months later an encounter with the woman he'd marry. He didn't divine she would remain the following years. He didn't anticipate fathering three children who would overlook his inadequacies and phone each Sunday after they left home. Apprehending these things would have been a relief, yes, but a distraction.

A seer's gift isn't the extent of his vision, Yeller determined, it's how thoroughly you includes yourself in the minute you're in. Anyone could forecast the next sunrise or that in 7 billion years it would explode. A volcano's eruption, though, anticipating that requires your whole presence. Yeller was uncertain how he'd managed such a feat. He was unsure he could repeat it but even wondering that seemed staring too far up the road.

Later in the ashy pall, Yeller encountered the woman from his biology class. Her body bent forward, head down as if she were a drill bit boring through all this. She persisted past him, oblivious to those around her attempting to press ash into something they could throw or others making themselves angels as they had as children in snow.

He imagined her possessing the pencil still, perhaps for notes in other classes or to-do lists or parents' correspondence. But how did all her scratching and erasing serve her? She balanced equations and simplified functions, yet she had not discerned what Yeller had: There would be no midterm.

She marched away from Yeller and the revelers, whose shadows, flattened by the opaque light and the heaviest sky imaginable, were liberated from such ordinary concerns. She could not hear their laughter – not drunken or cynical – this laughter was the laughter of children, babies even, as if the others with him were remembering just now grace is everywhere.

 Bruce Holbert, a retired Mt. Spokane High School English teacher, is the author of three novels. His second, *The Hour of Lead* (Counterpoint Press), won the Washington State Book Award for fiction. His latest, *Whiskey* (Picador), was released in 2018. A graduate of the Iowa Writers Workshop, Holbert's fiction and essays have appeared in the *Iowa Review*, the *Antioch Review*, the *New Orleans Review*, the *Sante Fe Writers Project*, *River* and the *New York Times*.

Miriam and Clara, 1980

Johanna Stoberock

Clara was 15, but when Miriam looked at her, she could see her as a baby still. She'd been a fat baby, and Miriam had complained endlessly about what it felt like to carry her – aching back, aching shoulders, constantly wrestling with an animal that wouldn't take responsibility for its own weight. But now, now she'd give anything for those clearly assignable aches, anything to have her baby press a fat cheek into her face, slobbering her baby slobber onto Miriam's skin.

Maybe they'd made a mistake, only having one baby. She'd always had enough, though, with Clara. She had enough holding her little girl's hand and chatting with her before bed and brushing her hair while she squirmed and squirmed and then screamed. Miriam hadn't known she'd be able to be cruel, before she became a mother. She didn't know she had it in her, that everyday cruelty of turning an animal child into a human being. But she was capable. She'd even come to see the cruelty of taming as a kind of strength.

And now? Now Clara wouldn't give her the time of day.

Bill told her to wait. He told her all kids vanish when they hit a certain age. "Give her time," he said. "She's just figuring herself out. Kids do that. She'll come back."

He was right. Miriam knew he was right. But it was different between Clara and her. For one thing, Bill had a life beyond their house. When Clara was born, they'd decided Miriam would stay home with her. Miriam hadn't ever really liked working anyway. And child care cost so much that it seemed like, as long as they could afford it, it made sense for her to be a full-time mom.

Clara sat at the table now eating a bowl of cereal. Her hair was black. That was new. It had happened secretly overnight. Her nails were green. She was chewing in time to some private music in her head. She used to hum when she ate. So sweet. Kids at school had teased her about it, but Miriam had never wanted her to stop. She didn't hum out loud anymore, but it seemed like there was always some rhythm circling around inside her that Miriam could see but not find inside herself.

"Do you need a ride home from school?" Miriam said.

Clara didn't move. Had she even heard her?

"I could pick you up. Happy to do it."

Clara kept chewing.

"Your loss," Miriam said.

Clara shrugged. She left the house to wait for the bus without saying goodbye. Miriam watched her through the window. Her daughter, visible as always, but barely recognizable.

The news was filled with talk of the mountain erupting. Three hundred miles from their eastern corner of the state, so far away it was hard to imagine that it mattered. But every night, scientists got on the TV with warnings. Violence was coming. Fire and molten rock. The scientists knew it would happen even if they didn't know exactly when. "Prepare yourself," they said. "Get to safety. Don't stay." Miriam didn't think they could possibly be speaking to her – 300 miles. So far away. But it felt like there was something personal about those warnings. She just couldn't figure out what.

It was hard to think of mountains, at least mountains here, in the Northwest, as volcanoes. Volcanoes were supposed to be on tropical islands. They were supposed to send showers of sparks into the air like fireworks, and their hot lava was supposed to travel down to the ocean in thick, glowing threads, and anybody who lived close to them was supposed to have already figured out how to organize their lives around the regular eruptions. Driving west, the giant mountains punctuating the Cascades seemed like ghosts. Mount Hood never appeared gradually. It was always just suddenly there, floating, white and from another world.

Or Mount Adams, just past Yakima: Sometimes she'd get a sideways glimpse of it, and then when she looked directly, it would be gone. Or Mount Rainier. In Seattle – when she was in college, when she'd met Bill – they used to joke about Rainier haunting them. It seemed like you'd be looking at the horizon and it would be empty, and then you'd turn away for a second and when you looked back the mountain would be there, covered in snow, larger than a mountain should be, like some kind of sign waiting to be read. But a sign of what? She'd loved its unknown quality then, that sense of something so much larger than the rest of the world, so resonant with meaning in its cold, stony way, but so impossible to understand.

She'd never been to Mount St. Helens. She wasn't sure she'd ever even seen it. But she imagined it the same as those other ghostly giants – snow-covered, appearing and disappearing at will, a sign of something more than a place itself, a sign that refused to surrender meaning.

She could use a sign now, she thought.

May was beautiful. Miriam's father had always said that the first week of May was when you could trust that every tree would have its leaves, and now, just past the first week, she couldn't stop thinking about him. The kind of green that settled from on high was pale and aching with life. The last time she'd seen her father, his hands had looked bleached, like old leaves, veins visible, the skin nearly rubbed off. And now, barely a year since his passing, she felt him everywhere.

I was 15 once, she thought. Did I seem ready to erupt in the same way that Clara does? She tried to remember back to when she was a kid. It had been her and her father alone. Had he watched her eat breakfast before heading off to school? She remembered sitting at the table by herself. She remembered the house mostly dark at night, just the light in her bedroom while she finished her schoolwork. The world had been quieter then. She asked Bill what he remembered from his childhood, and he just shook his head. If only her father was still alive. If only she could ask him what it had felt like to be her father, when she was still a child. If only she could ask him whether he'd waited for a sign, as well.

Clara had started taking walks at night. Miriam couldn't think of a reason to tell her no. After dinner, Clara would clear her plate, go to her room and then come back into the kitchen and say, "I'm going out for a while." Then the door would shut behind her.

"Say something to her," Miriam said to Bill. But when he tried, Clara just looked at him, and the longer she looked, the more he forgot what he wanted to say.

"Stand up to her," Miriam said.

"What's there to stand up to her about?" he said. "She's taking a walk. We don't want her to feel like a prisoner here. We don't want her to feel like we're her enemies."

"She's ours to protect," Miriam said.

"She's ours to trust," Bill said.

On a Saturday night in mid-May, the heads on the television were practically screaming. The earth was about to split open. Walls of rock would turn liquid. Fire would blaze. Ash would be pushed up into the sky so thick and heavy that it would cover the sun and turn day to night.

"These are not predictions," Miriam heard. "These are facts. This is science. This is real."

And outside, the street lamps glowed the same soft light they always glowed.

"I'm going out," Clara said.

Miriam looked at Bill. Bill looked at the television. The scientists looked back, opened their mouths, practically screaming their warnings.

The door shut softly. Just a month ago, it would have slammed. But now Clara seemed more interested in slipping away than in announcing her departure with a bang. The night was cold. Miriam could feel the chill sneaking in. She grabbed Clara's jacket and ran out behind her. Her daughter needed freedom, but she didn't need to be cold while she was looking for it.

But Clara wasn't anywhere. Not on the sidewalks lit in circles by the streetlamps. Not down the street where the town ended and the county began and streetlamps gave way to front porch lights that as usual were mostly turned off. Night had fallen. It was dark now in the world, dark and her daughter was gone.

Miriam moved quickly, certain that she was moving faster than Clara would be, certain that wherever her daughter might be going, she would be able find her, would overtake her, would make sure she was safe. A mother should be able to do that. Her daughter was ahead of her, as certain as any vision she'd ever had.

But she didn't find her. The night stayed dark.

Up ahead, the road turned into a bridge that crossed the creek. They used to spend hours there tossing pine cones into the water and watching them float away. Miriam stopped on the bridge, out of breath, and leaned against the cement railing. She could hear the water down below, though at first she couldn't see it – it seemed that all the different darknesses of night blended together here.

But the longer she looked, the more she was certain that a part of the darkness was changing shape. Bring my daughter back, bring my daughter back, please bring my daughter back: The words rattled in her head, and she imagined the black water taking her words away, carrying them onward to an invisible part of the world that might or might not listen.

When she got home, Bill shrugged and nodded his head toward Clara's bedroom door, closed, as always.

The mountain erupted at 8:30 the next morning, power beyond imagining.

Then quiet.

And then, at 11a.m., 300 miles away, ash began to fall.

Miriam banged on Clara's bedroom door and Clara opened it, rubbing sleep from her eyes, a scowl already settled on her face.

"Get dressed," Miriam said.

And Clara did.

The two of them stepped out onto the street, ash falling around them like snow, piling and piling up in the warm May day, as soft as feathers, as soft as a mother's touch. The new green leaves disappeared, covered by inches of dust. But underneath, underneath there somewhere, Miriam knew there was green still, and for just that moment she trusted that it would emerge again, and when it did she would forget all this and remember that the condition of the world is meant to be joy.

 Johanna Stoberock is the author of the novels *Pigs* (Red Hen Press) and *City of Ghosts* (W.W. Norton). The 2019 recipient of the Artist Trust/Gar LaSalle Storyteller Award, 2016 Runner Up for the Italo Calvino Prize for Fiction and a 2012 Jack Straw Fellow, Stoberock's work has appeared in the *Chicago Review of Books*, *Lit Hub*, the *Best of the Net Anthology* and elsewhere. She lives in Walla Walla, where she teaches in the Composition and First Year programs at Whitman College.

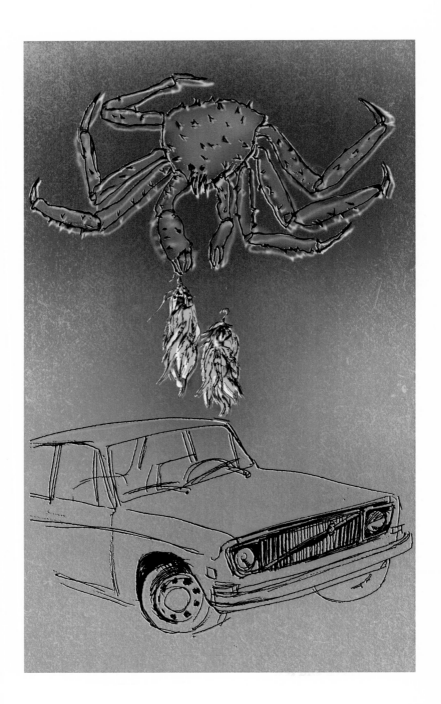

Waffle Hut

Neal Thompson

I saw my twin sister working at the Waffle Hut outside Kid Valley, her hair longer and grayer since we last spoke. That was nine years back, when mom died. An aneurysm seemed to have been waiting and waiting for just the right moment, and then POP! Mom's gone. Sixty-seven and healthier than either of us, knocked to the ground by a tiny gremlin, right there outside the Goodwill.

I didn't think my sister saw me, but I was wrong. I was usually wrong about Ellen.

Two weeks later, when I finally got up the nerve to return, I was sitting in a Waffle Hut booth and she was filling my coffee cup like I was any old customer. "What can I get you, Danny?" she said.

"Oh, it's just Dan, now," was all I could say.

"OK then," she said. "*Dan.*"

"I saw you the other day," she said as I pretended to read the menu. "Still driving dad's Volvo, I see?"

Ah, the Volvo. I'm an idiot.

"Yeah," I said. "I always hated that heap, but now I can't seem to get rid of it – 257,000 miles and counting."

"I'll bring you some eggs," she said. "I get off at 2 if you want to come back and tell me why you're stalking me."

We met that afternoon at the Twin Peaks Tavern in Castle Rock, sat by the window on a clear day gifting us with a glittery display of the jagged Cascade peaks to the east. I told her what I'd come to say: I had cancer, and it didn't look good. None of me looked good.

Twenty-two months behind bars in Yakima hadn't helped. Neither had slipping into the icy Bering Sea off the *Janie J.*, and just as I was starting to make some real money from them gangly Alaskan crabs. Nothing ever seemed to work out the way I pictured it up front. But I guess it didn't work out much better for her, either. I mean ... the Waffle Hut?

Out of her apron, she looked good. Better than a waitress and way better than me. I'd started lazing into a Crocs and sweatpants look – easier on my back without laces and belts. A Sonics cap to cover what's left of my hair. But Ellen always had this Indian style. Dangly feather earrings, turquoise on her fingers and wrists. Today she wore a colorful vest, hiking shorts and running shoes. She had tan legs that looked strong. She'd be that fit, cool, mystical aunt if I'd managed to have kids.

"What really brings you back home then, Dan? Still with that Madeline?"

She never did like my wife, now my ex. I told her first about the *Janie J.*, how four crew mates and the skipper went down so fast, but I somehow made it to the life raft and survived the night, except for three toes lost to frostbite and numb spots on my face. She said she'd read about it in the papers, saw my picture.

"Maddy left me after that," I said. "Told me I wasn't right. And I guess I was drinking more than usual."

I didn't talk about what came next: the coke, trying to find money for coke, robbing a food truck in Tacoma, the two-year sentence, minus two months for good-enough behavior. Though I'd quit smoking over a year ago, my right hand started twitching, sensing the ghost limb of a Marlboro Red.

She just nodded.

I told her I'd heard about her day in the news, sole survivor of an avalanche on the back flanks of Silver Mountain, which killed two of her friends and a snowboarder. "It's weird, right?" I said, peeling the label off my bottle to keep my hands busy. "We're both, like, survivors. But ... but not really, I guess."

She nodded again, ordered two more beers. Asked again: "Why'd you come back, Danny boy?"

I wanted to tell her it felt like getting pulled toward the scene of a car wreck, knowing the injured and the dead had been hauled away already, but still curious about the spot. … Did the cops miss anything? A CD, a library card, sunglasses, a shoe? What did it feel like to stand in that place? Did it hum?

Instead, inevitably, we got around to the day dad died, coming up on 30 years now – the date just a few weeks away, the newspapers probably working on their anniversary stories. We talked about dad, stubborn as granite, refusing to come down off the mountain, a hero to other folks who thought the government was overreacting with its evacuation plans. How she and I were a hundred miles away, at Pike Place Market, less than 20 yards apart from each other when it blew, took dad from us.

"I was, like, halfway into my shift at the fish market, nursing a killer hangover and about to get fired. You were down in that stairwell, trying to sing, I think, Bruce Springsteen with that ponytailed Indi–"

"Native," she jumped in.

"Yes, OK , right, that *Native* boyfriend of yours … that jerk."

She made an exasperated lippy horse-like sound, then kept tearing open sugar packets, pouring them into hills of sugar. "First off," she finally said. "We were singing Van the Man, not Bruce. And second, we didn't start singing till later, after we'd heard the news."

"Whatever."

The day after the explosion, as we called it, when we couldn't reach Mom or Dad, I'd given Ellen and her boyfriend a ride back home. We found Mom the next day at a FEMA shelter in a lumber camp. It was all so unrecognizable. So much mud and rock and ash and muck. Everything we'd ever known looked broken, spoiled, flung about, gray and melted and dangerous. Thirteen-hundred feet of mountaintop, just gone.

I couldn't stop thinking: Is he up there somewhere? But he was gone for good, which was maybe his plan. Too close to the danger zone, the authorities said. Didn't have a chance. They found around half the bodies, but Dad and the rest? I often wondered how it ended. … Did he evaporate? Was he trapped in mud? Would archaeologists find him thousands of years later, body intact, his mouth open in a scream or a laugh?

Ellen and I had been close as kids, but after the explosion we drifted apart. It felt like we were all stuck in mud, stuck in time, and we both moved away from that scarred, wrecked place. I guess that's what I'd loved about being on the water. Nothing solid. Open space. Soft and salty liquid. Just floating.

A week after my drinks with Ellen, I started my first rounds of chemo and radiation. Everything slowed to a sludgy crawl. And after a month I just knew: I didn't have what it took to beat this. I didn't have the strength.

I'd been living alone in this old abandoned boat up on blocks in my buddy Willem's backyard. But after seeing my sister — and, honestly, after the rats invaded my boat — I decided to move into a tiny apartment near Ellen, closer to home, even though I hated being in the shadow of that ruined, shrunken mountain.

A month later, my body beginning to shrink from the chemo, I called her. Our birthday was the next week.

"Should we drive up and see? Maybe next Wednesday?"

She knew what I meant, and said, "You mean what's left of it?"

It felt like she was waiting for me, or someone, to ask.

"I've never been back," she said. "Not even close."

"Me, neither," I said. "OK, then? Let's do it?"

I'd read once — probably in one of those anniversary stories — that people living near disaster areas suffered from stress, depression, insomnia, anxiety, irritability, a sense of powerlessness. I wanted to ask Ellen about that. Could she sleep? Was she anxious? Angry? But driving east on Highway 504 in dad's Volvo, listening to Dylan's "Lay Lady Lay" on the radio, she started singing along. So I asked ...

"Why'd you stop playing music back then?"

She'd always had a pretty voice. I hadn't appreciated it during those few weeks when she was busking at Pike Place and I was working upstairs at the fish market, throwing salmon for the tourists and making money and meeting girls, on the verge of saving enough to escape somewhere new.

She looked at me like I was an idiot.

"I ... I didn't," she said. "I never stopped. Didn't you get the CDs I sent?"

"You sent me CDs?" I tried to keep my eyes on the road – Spirit Lake Highway, they called it now – as it started swerving and the mountain kept popping up between the folds to our right, and I began to feel dizzy.

"Dude, I had a band for years. The Mountain Mommas? We started out as Crater Face, but that sounded too punk so we countrified our name and our songs. We just played covers – Eagles, Dead, Neil Young, that kind of thing, bar band tunes. But I loved it – bars, casinos, VFWs, ski areas. A couple festivals."

"We actually played this one," she said, as Springsteen came on, and she started singing along.

Everything dies baby that's a fact
But maybe everything that dies someday comes back

"That's cool, Sissy," I said, using the old nickname. "I'd love to come see you play some–"

"Don't, Danny."

"–time."

"Just, don't ... Don't call me that?"

"Call you what? Sissy?"

"Yeah, that."

Bruce kept singing:

Now our luck may have died and our love may be cold, but with
you forever I'll stay

"Cuz I'm not, you know. Didn't you know? Didn't mom ever tell you? I never asked her."

For some reason, right then I thought about our father's alleged final words, captured over the short-wave radio as the eruption began. "This is it!" he'd yelled, and I always wondered what he was thinking.

I wanted to ask her about that, but I turned off the radio and asked, "You're not ... not what?"

"Your sister."

Months later, near what felt like the end, I was living in Ellen's spare bedroom, fuzzy from the morphine and my body like one big, throbbing ache. I woke up one night, moaning, convinced I was done for.

"This is it," I told Ellen, who came and sat by my side. But she just scoffed.

"Knock it off, Dan. Don't be so dramatic. You sound just like Dad."

Neal Thompson is the author of five books, most recently the memoir, *Kickflip Boys* (Ecco). He has written for *Esquire*, *Outside*, the *New York Times*, and *Washington Post*. His forthcoming book is *The First Kennedys: An Immigrant Maid, Her Bartender Son, and the Humble Roots of a Dynasty*, due out from Houghton Mifflin Harcourt in 2021. He lives in Seattle with his family.

Fissures

Kris Dinnison

They were fighting again. They'd come to Seattle because her dad had a meeting, but Becky knew they also came because of the fighting.

"I have to go to Seattle for a few days for business," he'd said last week. "I'll be back Sunday night."

"Sure. Go. I'll just stay here and wait for you. That sounds like a dream come true." Her mom's voice was sweet. But Becky knew from experience it also was sticky. A trap.

"Joanne, the counselor, said sarcasm isn't an effective way for us to communicate our feelings."

Her mom had thrown a fit and a few breakable items from the hall bookcase. "Is that direct enough for you, Dennis?"

After narrowly dodging a crystal ashtray that likely would have brained him, he suggested they all go to Seattle, a family weekend.

"It'll be fun," he said.

But now they were at each other. Again. This was out-in-public fighting: more whispering and hissed insults. Less shouting and throwing things and slamming doors. Becky hummed a tune, which she realized was *All Out Of Love* by Air Supply. She hated that song, but not as much as she hated their constant quarreling.

Becky drifted away from their buzzing anger, still humming that terrible song. She'd read the revolving floor of the Space Needle made one complete rotation in 47 minutes. If she moved to the other side of the circle, could she just rotate around and around and never see her parents again?

"Becky," her mother's voice rang sharp among the crowd of tourists. "Stay close."

Becky's shoulders slumped. "And stand up straight."

Becky began humming again and leaned her forehead against the cool glass trying to see over the edge. She knew they were spinning, that the floor beneath them wasn't static. But the view didn't seem to change, or maybe it just changed so slowly she didn't notice. Her parents fighting was that way. When did they get like this? She wondered. Becky remembered being happy, she remembered them being happy. But maybe she was just too young and stupid to notice the change.

In the distance, past the skyscrapers, she could see Mount Rainier. And beyond that, she knew, were Mount Adams and Mount St. Helens. The volcano. They were all volcanoes, Becky knew, but Mount St. Helens wasn't squatted quietly in the Cascade Range minding its own business like the others. It had been grumbling and shifting for months. And they said on the news that the earthquakes were happening daily.

"Beckers," her dad put his hand on her shoulder. "Time to go."

Becky looked around for her mom, who stood in line for the elevator, her arms crossed, her mouth a stiff line. Becky saw her glance at her watch, then adjust it on her narrow wrist.

"We're going to be late for the zoo," she said as Becky joined her in line.

"You can't be late for the zoo, Mom."

"And where's your father gone to now?" She looked at her watch again, though only 30 seconds had passed since the last time.

"I'm right here," Becky's dad said.

"Dennis, could you please try not to wander off? I swear it's like you're the child instead of Becky."

"I'm not a child," Becky muttered.

Dennis put an arm around his wife's shoulders. "Joanne, relax. This is supposed to be fun." Joanne shrugged out from under Dennis' arm. Becky saw his smile slide, then harden. "Well then, could you at least try not to make everyone miserable?"

Joanne scowled at him. "I learned from the best."

Later, at the zoo, Becky's mom dragged them from the giraffes to the big cats to the chimpanzees. Becky wasn't sure if it was actual enthusiasm or some sort of internal, unspoken itinerary that drove Joanne.

"Did you know chimpanzees actually make and use tools?" Joanne said, shading her eyes and peering at the enclosure.

"Did you know chimpanzees will sometimes eat each other's babies?" Becky asked.

Her mother stared at her. "You really are awful sometimes, Rebecca. Why do you have to ruin things?"

"I learned from the best," Becky said.

Joanne's nostrils flared. She turned and stomped toward the zoo exit.

"Nice," Dennis said. "Very nice."

"What?" Becky shrugged. "I read it in *National Geographic*."

Her father dropped his head, then followed Joanne. Becky turned back to the chimps for a few minutes, watching. Three chimps groomed each other under a tree, and two younger ones swung and chased each other around a pile of boulders. One chimp sat alone watching her. Becky waved to him, but instead of waving back, the chimp showed his teeth, then made a loud hooting sound. Becky couldn't shake the idea that he was laughing at her.

The rest of the day and evening did not improve. There was the moment when Dennis drove their giant station wagon onto the freeway going north instead of south because Joanne was holding the map upside down and the moment when Joanne sent her wine back three times, something that made Dennis and Becky want to sink into the restaurant booth and disappear. And, finally, there was the

moment when her parents had another whisper fight in front of the
hotel clerk about, of all things, what time they'd be leaving in the
morning. Joanne was all for an early alarm clock and getting on the
road by 8. Dennis wanted to sleep in and eat breakfast at a nearby
diner.

Becky wanted to suddenly develop laser eyes, aim them at her
parents and vaporize both of them. Instead, she hummed, and she
could see the poor clerk didn't know which was worse: the bickering
hotel guests or their strange, murmuring daughter.

Sunday morning her father got his way by accident when the
alarm on the hotel clock radio didn't go off. Becky woke with a start
and glanced at her watch: 8:32.

"Did you turn it off on purpose?" Joanne asked Dennis as they
packed their bags.

"Christsakes, Joanne. Of course not," Dennis said.

Becky began to dread the drive home: six hours of forced confine-
ment with these people. Six more years of living with them. Sometimes she wished they'd finally just have the big fight instead of these
skirmishes. That one of them would blow a hole in their marriage that
couldn't be repaired. But they never did. So they all lived in dread and
longing, waiting for that day.

To Becky's relief, they didn't speak through breakfast, didn't speak
as Dennis wound through downtown trying to find the freeway on
ramp, didn't speak until they were almost in Issaquah, when traffic
began to slow and then stop. Becky craned her neck and could see
emergency lights ahead, and there was a state patrolman making his
way down the line of cars, leaning into each window, after which the
driver would turn on the blinker and move to the off-ramp.

When he reached their car, Dennis rolled down the window.

"What is it," he asked. "An accident? How long is the delay?"

"Sorry, sir, but the pass is closed until further notice."

"What? Why? I have to get back for work in the morning."

The patrolman looked at Becky's dad and kind of laughed. "You
haven't heard?"

Joanne leaned over. "Heard what?"

"St. Helens blew her top this morning," the man said. "The whole side of the mountain came off, and the ash cloud is moving east. Visibility is so bad they closed I-90."

"When will it open again?" Dennis asked.

"No idea, Mister. You'll have to exit here and either find a place to stay or head back west." He patted his hand on the top of the car and stood up. "Be safe."

Becky's dad turned on his blinker and eased the car off the highway and into Issaquah. Traffic was backed up, each motel they passed already had their "no vacancy" signs lit. He pulled the station wagon into a grocery parking lot and turned off the motor.

"Why are you stopping?" Joanne asked.

Dennis turned to her, then looked back at Becky. "An actual volcano," he said. "Can you believe it?" He shook his head. "I never imagined I'd see the day."

The three of them sat for a minute. Becky considered the scientific words she'd learned to describe an event like this: magma, ash, lava, fissure. But none of them seemed enough to contain the wonder she heard in her father's voice.

Becky's mom smiled for the first time that day. "What do we do now?"

"We head south."

"Dennis, that's toward the mountain," she said.

"Joanne, a volcano erupted. I'm pretty sure that's the worst thing that's going to happen today." He grabbed her hand. "Trust me?"

Becky saw her mom poised at the edge of an argument for just a moment, then saw her step away from that edge. "OK," she laughed. "Why not? Let's go south."

Dennis turned the car around, winding southwest through the hills, then onto the interstate. Her parents didn't fight the whole way. They talked about the mountain. They listened to the news on the radio. They shook their heads, smiled at each other, repeatedly amazed at the miracle of a volcano, an actual volcano, erupting just 50 miles away. Becky wasn't sure what to do with the marvel of her parents going hours without squabbling. She didn't have to hum at all. Not once all day. It was disorienting. It was wonderful.

Becky watched carefully from the back seat, but the mountain never showed itself, and her parents never fought. Night was falling as they crossed the Columbia River into Oregon. They stopped for gas, and her mom made a bed out of their coats and an old blanket they always kept in the car.

"Can we roll down the back window?" Becky asked as she settled into the nest.

Her mom smiled. "Sure. But let me know if you get too cold."

Laying in the back of the station wagon, Becky watched the sky go dark. Her parents' voices, pitched low and soft, floated toward her from the front seat. She hung her feet out the window, the cool air whipping around her bare toes. Looking at the stars in the clear sky, it was hard to remember that just a few hours ago, a mountain had exploded nearby.

Becky imagined when they got back to Spokane the entire city would be gray, nothing spared from the layer of fine ash. And people had died; she'd heard that on the radio. She knew the eruption wasn't a good thing. But today the mountain made her parents smile at each other for the first time in months: something beautiful in the devastation.

 Kris Dinnison of Spokane is a former teacher, a small business owner, and author of the novel *You and Me and Him* (HMH Books for Young Readers). Her writing has appeared in *The Spokesman-Review*, *London Journal of Fiction*, *One Teen Story*, and the *Young Adult Review Network*.

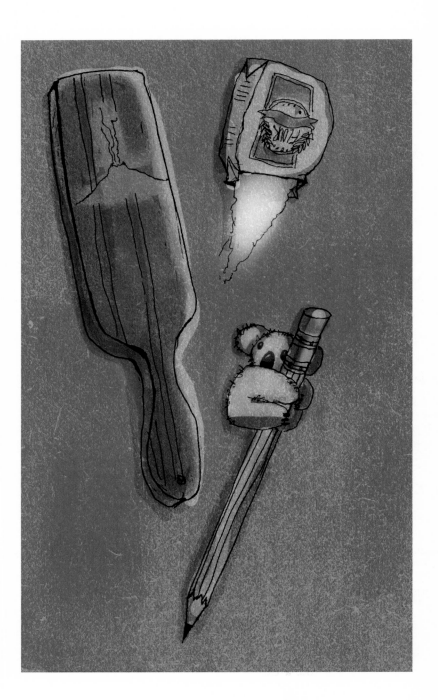

Peebags for Manboy

Matthew Sullivan

I. Rumblings

Our big sister Theresa ran away forever on the day that we climbed onto the roof and threw sandwich baggies of hot pee at her boyfriend. Her disappearance wasn't part of the plan, and the three of us definitely paid for what we did.

But if ever a guy deserved to be hit with bags of hot pee, it was him. Manboy, we called him. He worked as a dishwasher and got kicked out of school for selling weed, which was fine with us, but he had a mustache and looked more like her uncle than her boyfriend, which was not fine with us at all.

Theresa was barely even a freshman in high school, a few years older than us.

Our parents must have thought Manboy was creepy, too, because they banned him from coming around when Dad wasn't home. Theresa's response was to devise a system in which Manboy would drive by our house in his powder-blue Chevette and then she'd pretend to take our dog for a walk. He'd park in the shade of a Winnebago up the block, and she'd throw the dog in the back of his car and then they'd …

In truth, we had no idea what they were up to in his broiling Chevette, which was why we commando crawled single file through the gutter – bare feet, gym shorts, no shirts – until we spotted his car, standing out like a tropical fish on our drab street. We slipped into the closest lawn and ripped up all the grass our fists could hold. We stooped near the wheel wells and, on three, burst up and threw handfuls of grass into the windows and ...

Oh.

We were expecting to catch them smoking a cigarette or whispering about Lovely Love, but instead we caught them Frenching.

Really Frenching.

We stared at our bare feet, unable to move, until our dog jumped out of the car window and broke our trance.

We'd been planning Manboy's demise ever since their first date, but the plan had always been abstract – until now.

We sprinted straight home and gathered supplies. We leaned a ladder against our house and scrambled onto the roof. Our bladders thrummed as we wizzed into sandwich baggies, the cheap kind that folded over.

We could hear Manboy's Chevette revving through the neighborhood. The car had hardly even braked to a halt before Theresa was running toward the porch with grass in her hair, yelling.

"Mom!"

Maybe she'd assumed we were already inside telling Mom, and she was hoping to cut us off, to concoct a scenario in which Manboy had needed CPR or something – anything but Frenching.

Manboy ran toward the house behind Theresa as if his presence might help her cause. He was even stupider than we'd thought.

We stood directly over the porch, shingles warm beneath our toes. Our baggies of pee were briny and alive, like something in the jellyfish family.

"Hey, Manboy. Up here!"

He stopped in his tracks and bombs away: Our three hot baggies hit him with military accuracy, two on the head, one on the shoulder.

All three sloshed open on impact. He got pretty dripping wet, but that was just phase one of our plan: the Pee Drench.

Phase two happened when he was spinning around on the driveway below, spitting and clawing at his eyes. That's when we leaned over the roof with the 5-pound sack of flour. We sucked in school, but we were really good planners.

The idea was that this storm of powder would mingle with the pee and turn Manboy into a doughy yellow monster caked with a paste that was impossible to clean off. We'd imagined the flour taking the shape of a cloud as it fell, billowing around him and swallowing him in its poof.

Only it didn't happen like that: Seconds after we upended the sack, he looked up and the flour came crashing down not as a cloud, but as a cylinder, holding the form it had in the sack, and clobbered him between the eyes.

We sucked air through our teeth: Ouch!

He stumbled toward the porch, gasping like a mummy in a horror film, no doubt terrified of what might drop next.

Mom and Theresa came rushing out. Mom first saw him, then she saw her flour spilled on the driveway like crime scene chalk. As Mom wiped his eyes and performed triage on his ego, Theresa screeched at the sky. Particles of flour circled through the air like ash.

"Get down here!" Mom said.

We refused. No good could come of that.

We watched her walk to the side of the house and lower the ladder to the grass.

"Your father's on his way."

They went inside and closed the door. Then we heard the ungodly sound of Mom walking through the house, closing all of the windows, as if to minimize the reach of our screams.

Whoosh, slam.

She knew what was coming.

The giant had been awakened.

II. Apocalypse

We spent all afternoon stranded on the roof watching shadows shift, waiting for our father.

He had a collection of leather belts in a rainbow of colors, and each performed its duty well, but by the time we were in grade school, they no longer contained the presence he was after in his punishments. He invited an old bread board into the arsenal and seemed pleased by the way it was soon scarred by sliced toast and denim rivets, seasoned by skin and tears.

When the bread board splintered one Sunday morning, Dad went to the lumber yard and bought a slab of black walnut, then he spent the entire day fashioning a new paddle in the garage. Mom said it was a healthy way to focus his energy, but our souls withered with each swish of sandpaper, each ping of the chisel. When it was finished, he swung it through the air with admiration, his hairy knuckles twitching in the breeze.

The dread we felt was temporarily broken when Manboy came out of the house alone and wogged to his Chevette, holding a bag of frozen peas to the bridge of his nose.

We were miserable but couldn't resist.

"Hey, Manboy! You got peas on your face!"

As he drove away, we yelled loud enough to ward off any potential suitors.

"Next time we cut out your tongue!"

Somewhere below us, we could hear Theresa roaring about the injustice of being born.

"You," Mom yelled back, "are in even worse trouble than your brothers!"

We felt bad for Theresa. She soon stormed out hugging a paper grocery bag, her clothes spilling across the driveway like the remnants of an evacuation.

"Where are you going?" we said, worried.

"Anywhere but here," she said, looking at the sky. "Dad is coming, you idiots!"

"Take us with you?" we said, but she was gone.

We sweltered up there, curling into the shade. We tried to pretend we were birds but were too old, so we just felt worse.

Five-thirty came around. We could sense our father climbing into his station wagon 17 miles away, his rage already trembling within the house, through its pipes and wires.

We hid behind the ridge as he parked and climbed out of the car. He poked the flour in the driveway with his toe. Without looking up, he leaned the ladder against the gutter, then quietly went inside.

He was giving us a choice: Climb down and run away, as Theresa had, or climb down and face him.

By the time we approached the front door – single file like a centipede, all sobbing as one – he was sitting on the porch waiting with a cracked belt on one thigh, his walnut paddle on the other.

His eyes glowed red. We'd never seen him happier.

III. Aftermath

Many months passed, and Theresa just never came home.

We could still smell her perfume in the bathroom, and her hairbrush still jammed the drawer each time we tried to find a Q-Tip.

One day at the mall, when we were shoplifting king-sized chocolate bars for our teachers, we saw Theresa walking head down carrying a maroon apron in her fist. Our first thought was to tackle her before she disappeared again, but instead we followed her from a distance.

We trailed her past the fountains, past the old men smoking indoors, and ended up at a country buffet place with a sign that said Roast Beef 'n Juice $5.95! She tied on the apron.

We came up with a plan – a nice plan, not one with baggies of pee. At the Hallmark store, we bought a greeting card and the smallest stuffed animal in the world, a fuzzy koala that clipped to the end of your pencil.

The card said, "I'm sorry," and underneath it we wrote "We're sorry for what we did" to Manboy.

We signed it carefully:

Mark O'Connor

John O'Connor

Luke O'Connor

Back at the restaurant, we sat in a booth far away from all the drooling geezers. We were unsure whether Theresa would fly into a rage the way she used to, so we placed the card and the koala in full view. Soon she walked up with a tray and slid three Cokes before us. She was wearing a lot of makeup. She sat down and lit a cigarette.

She asked how we were holding up, and we shrugged. She laughed and said she stopped seeing Manboy not long after the ambush, and we were lucky he hadn't killed us. She asked about Mom, and we told her she seemed fine, but when we started saying Dad, she held up her hand.

"I don't want to hear about Dad."

We slid the card and koala across to her.

"Awww."

She opened the card, and her smile went away. She took a deep breath.

"Listen. Guys. You don't need to apologize. It's not your fault."

We didn't understand. It was our fault, we told her. Bags of pee didn't just fall from the sky.

"I'm sorry I left you guys there. I just couldn't take you with me."

We still didn't understand.

She put out her cigarette and leaned forward and gripped our wrists together like a bundle of flowers.

"It might feel like you don't have a choice," she said, "but you do. There are so many ways to be. He's just one out of many, many ways, OK?"

Now we really didn't understand.

Theresa took a pen out of her apron and clipped the koala to it. She opened the card, concentrating just like she used to when we did homework together after school. Then she crossed out our last name, whirling dark clouds across it until it completely disappeared.

"There," she said, and we felt the world go quiet. "See? Poof. He's gone."

 Matthew Sullivan's novel, *Midnight at the Bright Ideas Bookstore* (Scribner), won the 2018 Colorado Book Award and was an IndieNext pick and a GoodReads Choice Awards finalist. His writing has appeared in the *New York Times*, the *Daily Beast*, *LitHub* and elsewhere. He recently relocated from Central Washington to Anacortes, where he is teaching online and working on a crime novel set in Soap Lake.

My Father's Ashes

Jamie Ford

My brother tells me that as a baby, on the day I said my first word, my father's voice was already hoarse from yelling at my mother. When I took my first steps as a toddler, stumbling into my sister's open arms, a warm embrace that I've tried to remember because I don't ever want to forget her, my dad already had a limp from diabetes. When my cousin taught me to ride a bike, a used Schwinn that looked as though it'd been salvaged in a house fire, my father drove off in our only car. He said he was leaving for good, that he was never coming back. I chased him down the middle of Fruitvale Boulevard, crying. I was young and scared. But everyone else knew better, even my father, because he didn't take anything with him and was back in time for dinner.

We sat around the table and passed rice and canned peas and spoke about how Billy Carter, the president's alcoholic brother, had received a $200,000 loan from Libya, how the Yankees' Billy Martin had punched a Minnesota marshmallow salesman in a bar fight and how Billy Joel once tried to kill himself by drinking furniture polish. There were a lot of Billies in the Yakima newspaper in 1980. But what we talked about most was Mount St. Helens and whether it might erupt, acting as though a bomb hadn't already gone off at home, turning our living room into ground zero. Even today, I think about the need for an emotional Geiger counter and how it would light up, crackling from decades of fallout. Reminding me that I still hadn't reached the half-life of my family's emotional decay.

As we ate, I kept glancing over to my mother. She didn't talk much in those days, and I could predict how the evening would go simply by watching her eyes. Even as a boy, I knew the look of being crushed, being loved, being trapped, being praised, the confounding highs and lows of a being a human yo-yo, and it was only a matter of time before the string got tangled or broke altogether from mishandling.

"I heard that scientists near St. Helens are detecting 10,000 tiny earthquakes a day. That's gotta mean something big," my brother said as he cut his steak and gave me half. I then cut a smaller piece and tucked it into my pocket to share with our dog Chongo. The scruffy, pipe cleaner of a mutt had climbed into the dumpster behind our takeout restaurant and couldn't escape. My father rescued him and brought him home. He didn't mind when I fed the dog because even he had a soft spot for strays.

"That's a load a hooey." My father, who dropped out of high school at 15 to join the Merchant Marine as a ship's cook, was unconvinced of the danger. "They're just scaring everyone to try and sell more newspapers. Oldest trick in the book."

Scaring everyone, I thought, as I watched my father's old, faded tattoos flex and distort as he waved his arms while he talked. His hands as leathery as catchers' mitts when they came down on the table to make a point, scarred from kitchen cleavers and low blood sugar. Burns from sesame oil splatting out of a cast-iron wok. If scaring people led to increased sales, I imagined my father must be the richest man in the world.

"Why would scientists lie? I think they're just – you know – trying to keep people safe. Keep tourists away, before they all go …" My brother made an explosion noise, his eyes wide as he looked at me. "Wanna go fishing, little brother? I know a good spot."

"We should go," my father laughed. "We don't even need to bring our poles. Just let the lava heat the water to a boil – poached carp, add some scallions and oyster sauce – like a four-star restaurant. And if the whole place blows up, that's fine, too. I'd rather be cremated anyway, have my ashes scattered, than be stuck in a hole in the ground."

"Worm food," my brother said. "Worm's gotta eat, too."

Watching my brother and father joke and laugh, I knew they loved each other as much as any father and son. Despite coming home from school last week and hearing a yelping sound in the backyard. I thought maybe Chongo had been hit by a car, or worse – got in a fight with the neighbor's one-eyed pit bull. But the sound had been coming from my brother. He was upright, pinned against the garage, his face pressed into the metal siding. My father had one hand on the back of my brother's neck, the other gripped a leather belt that he swung against bare skin, red with welts. My father, a lifelong chain-smoker, had caught my brother doing the same.

I wondered where my mother was. Why she never put a stop to anything? That night I took out the garbage and saw the empty bottles of vodka and Kahlua. Years later, I understood why she took so many naps at odd hours, so maybe she'd been sleeping.

As I heard another crack of the belt, my brother turned his head my way.

I ducked inside as fast as I could. Ran to my room. I locked the door and hid in my closet that smelled of old shoes and dead grass, hoping he was OK , but more that, I hoped he hadn't seen me. It's one thing to catch a beating, but there's another pain, the one that comes from the embarrassment and humiliation of knowing someone else has seen you at your weakest, robbed of all your dignity.

"How about we all go fishing tomorrow? Bear Lake should be open," my father asked as he put chili oil on his rice that night at supper. "We can get up before dawn, get to the lakeshore just as the sun's coming up, that's when fish are biting."

I waited for my brother to answer because if he said yes, I might not have to go. I liked the idea of fishing more than the reality of getting up at 4 a.m. When the air was cold, the water chilly and the nightcrawlers my father used as bait were fresh. To be honest, the only reason I ever went fishing was for the Tootsie Rolls that my father kept in his tackle box. Though I did enjoy whenever my father invited one of the new cooks, like the skinny old man from China who didn't speak English. As soon as he caught a bass, he gutted the fish with a pocket knife, made a tiny fire, cooked and ate it right there on the shoreline. He gave me the cheek, the tenderest part, that melted in my mouth, and I realized that generosity exists everywhere, but especially in poverty.

"I have to go open the restaurant, get things ready," my brother said. He was only 14 but had already worked as a prep cook for two years. Soon I'd join him and my parents in the kitchen where he'd anoint me, King of the Dish Pit, the way my father had called him the same. My father had even made a paper crown for my brother and said, "This kingdom is now yours," as he pointed to a bus tub full of dirty pans covered in dried chow fun, black bean sauce and orange peels.

"Guess it's just you and me, kid," my father said, looking in my direction.

My mother met my gaze in a pregnant silence, and I realized, even as a third-grader, that her desire for a better life or at least a different one, had been stillborn. In that brief exchange, we wordlessly clung to each other like the living at a funeral.

"What … if I … don't really like fishing?" I asked, afraid of the answer.

My father looked at me as though I'd broken his heart, failed him as a son, betrayed him for a few extra hours of sleep. Or just as likely, he must have realized how scared I was of him. He just said, "Uh huh," and stared at my mother.

In that moment, I wondered if things would have been different if my sister still lived at home with us. She always liked to fish and had gone dozens of times with her boyfriend, right up until she'd been sent away.

I woke up that night to the unfinished symphony of my childhood. The sonata of slamming doors. The featured minuet of my mother crying. My father's usual, angry soliloquy about how she had turned everyone against him. My mother's vain pleas to not wake the kids. My father replying, "I'm not yelling. THIS IS YELLING."

As I plugged my ears, I looked out my bedroom window and saw a star. I drew a deep breath, closed my eyes and made a wish – for my mother, for my brother, for the sister that I knew I'd never see again – that my father might go away, once and for all. That the door would slam one last time and the car would speed away and not come back loaded with ice cream or a replacement TV from the Salvation Army.

In the morning, I woke to thunder, but as I got up, I didn't hear the sound of rain.

I found an empty place at the dining room table that normally would have been occupied by my father's chipped coffee mug, a copy of the Yakima Herald and an ashtray full of Camel cigarette butts. But all that remained of his presence was the collection of burns on the plastic tablecloth were he'd often set his smoke down for a minute too long.

I went to my parents' bedroom door, which had a fist-sized hole from an old argument. I peeked inside and saw the normal riot of dirty clothes, the broken mirror, the lamp without a shade, but my mother was alone, fast asleep. I stood for a moment and watched her breathe, her chest moving up and down, a liminal confirmation of life.

In the living room, I turned on the radio and listened to *Goodbye Stranger*.

I enjoyed the Sunday calm as I put on my shoes, my coat. Then the song was interrupted by the news, so I turned it off.

I went outside and rode my bike beneath a canopy of gray clouds, toward Elks Park, where I'd hoped to play whiffle ball with friends, or trade *Star Wars* cards, or laugh at who had stolen their father's chewing tobacco and gotten sick.

As I rode, I thought about my own father, wondering if and when he might return.

Then the sky began to darken, my nose felt itchy, my eyes watered, and when I looked up, my father's ashes were falling from the sky.

Jamie Ford is the great-grandson of Nevada mining pioneer, Min Chung, who emigrated from Kaiping, China to San Francisco in 1865, where he adopted the western name "Ford," thus confusing countless generations. His debut novel, *Hotel on the Corner of Bitter and Sweet* (Ballantine Books), spent two years on the *New York Times* bestseller list and went on to win the Asian/Pacific American Award for Literature, and has been optioned for film and stage. His second book, *Songs of Willow Frost* (Ballantine Books), was also a national bestseller. His work has been translated into 35 languages. His latest novel is *Love and Other Consolations Prizes* (Ballantine Books).

Volcanic

Deb Caletti

We've heard rumblings for two months, news of little earthquakes, hundreds of them. Explosions of steam, dark ash covering snow-clad summits. But let's be honest. I've heard rumblings for years. I know the signs: shivering teacups as a hand smacks a table. Explosions of steam you can feel, the heat coming right off his skin. Dark ash, a mood edging in. A shift in the atmosphere, a foreboding that makes you step oh-so-carefully, and turn the doorknobs oh-so-slowly.

There were eruptions, too. Bad enough that I had to clap my hands over my ears from the sound. I wanted to run but I couldn't, so I hid instead, though his rage always found me.

"Forget it, we're not going. Not when this place is worth $60,000, at least." Sean downs the last of his coffee, sets the cup on the deck. *This place*: our cabin, our home, just down the road from the lodge at Harmony Falls, along the curve of Spirit Lake. Those are beautiful words, *Harmony, Spirit*, and on that deck the mountain is *right there* across the water. It almost doesn't look real, the way it rises up so majestic, so powerful, bigger than anything around it by far, its own image rippling in the lake. It's strange the way something large and dangerous can almost make you feel safe until it doesn't. It's strange the way you can stare straight at it and know what it is but still ignore the warnings.

"Everything we have," I say. I rock and sway with the baby on my hip. I named him Will, because that's what you need to survive the world. One of his little socks is falling off, and I scoot it back up his chunky leg. I lean into him and smell the sticky peach scent of his cheeks.

"You don't just walk away from that." My husband doesn't like being told what to do. We've had this same conversation countless times. He leans back in his Adirondack chair. It's a beautiful morning, so why not. Spring. You can smell the drooping boughs of redwoods and the deepwater murkiness of the lake. His breakfast plate sits on the ground next to him, just bits of egg left, the overcooked parts, the thin skin from the sides of the pan. The slightly burnt edges of toast. He leaves behind the flawed parts, like a child would.

"It seems quiet," I say, watching that mountain. "It looks quiet." On my hip, Will jabbers his pretend-talk, and I gaze at him, and he gazes back with his endless-universe eyes. I tell him things that are only between us. Secret stuff. Like, the lie that I just spoke, because I don't think it looks quiet, not for one second. I can feel something building, down in the core, down in the dark parts no one can see. Silence isn't to be trusted, not that kind. For weeks now, I've seen that muscle working in Sean's neck, tightening, relaxing, tightening. I caught him pacing, and going stony, and I thought *uh oh*. I thought: *it's coming*. Sometimes eruptions aren't as personal as they seem. They're a collision forces that have little to do with you – stress, pressure, some instability that begins at the center and rises.

"It's fine! Fucking Dixy Lee Ray and her red zones. They told us Three Mile Island was the end of the world, too. If we took off, *we* would have had looters."

"Exactly," I say. But I don't really believe the Andelli's had looters. I think the door was open because they left in a hurry. That door was open because nothing inside mattered all that much, at the end of the day. All up and down Spirit Lake, those shingled houses, those charming little retreats – they're empty now. With the neighbors gone, I feel it more, the way the evergreens tower overhead, and the way the shady spots can get so cold, and the way the dark out there was deeper than any city dark. *Exactly* was a lie, too. It was helpful, all the years of practice, saying the things you needed to say to keep the mood even, feeding tidbits to his ego, turning down the temperature with your words. It was helpful to learn how to manipulate.

"The newspaper today? They said scientists who watch the mountain for a living aren't promising much of a show."

"See?" I say.

Inside, I wrestle that baby and change him, the little squirming, twisting guy. I smooch his bare belly. It's weird, because there's doom, doom everywhere, the heavy sense of imminent disaster, but I feel glee. I feel giddy, the way you do when something's almost over, or something's almost starting.

I try to take it all in – the crib with its rabbit bumper pads, the plants along the kitchen sill, the windows where you can see the fog roll in. But everything seems slippery, impossible to hold in memory. I'm too jittery with nerves maybe, or maybe sweet thoughts refuse to keep company with the others – the cowering in that corner, the hole punched in the wall over there, and in that room, his hand striking again and again as his face contorted in fury. I zip the keys to the truck into my pocket.

The baby naps, a small warm hump, diapered bottom up in the air, soft feather hair damp with sleep. I can hear him, Sean, chopping wood in the back. You know, for winter. For the future. I peek at him through the blinds. He has his Walkman clipped to his belt, his headphones on, probably the same cassette he listens to over and over. M-m-m-my Sharona! I can tell by the rhythm of the *thump, thump crack* of the ax. *Aye, aye, aye, whoo!*

I grab the important papers, the clothes, diapers, though, damn, babies come with so much stuff. I prop open the front screen with a rock so it doesn't bang shut. The chopping stops. I freeze, because no lie will cover this, what's gathered in my arms. The chopping starts again. I shove what I can under the seats.

That night, after Johnny Carson, he falls asleep on the couch. Dangerous – right in the living room. That mountain isn't going to wait for safe, though, and so I lift the baby, a heavy weight against my shoulder. I go out that front door, and I shut it carefully, and then I run. I run to the truck, and my heart is beating like crazy, and I'm going so fast, I lose a flip flop in the grass.

I toss Will into his little bucket. My hands are shaking so bad, I can barely get the key in. Then, *Rrr, rrr, rrr*, like a bad horror movie. It is one – one that began too long ago, when I was a lifetime younger. *Ooh my little pretty one, my pretty one! Aye, aye, aye, ooh!*

The engine turns, and I hit the gas, and we're down our road, and we're speeding under a midnight sky past those shingled houses, now empty. We're flying past Harmony Falls, and the old lodge, and we're taking the curves of Spirit Lake, the moon shining white, glittering the lake water, as that mountain looms. We drive the logging roads, the ones that go around the barricades set up weeks ago, keeping people out, keeping people in. It's so dark, and the roads are rough. We pass the Iron Creek Campground, and go over the bridge, and we're on Highway 12, but my eyes are on the rearview mirror the whole time, because I'm sure he's back there, following me in his dying Mustang. Every pair of headlights is him, I'm sure of it. I *feel* him, or maybe I just feel that mountain, inhaling, exhaling.

Any headlights behind us merge into a steady stream on I-5. What's everyone doing up so late? Who knows, but we're checking in to the River Inn in Chehalis. I have one shoe, but the woman says nothing. Shame floods in.

Behind that locked door, I make a call.

"We made it," I tell my brother.

My eyes burn with fatigue. A heart can't pound that hard and for that long without needing rest. Even here, between those pine-musty and unfamiliar sheets, with the baby beside me, I still feel him hovering. Finally, I drift into sleep.

The blast almost knocks me out of bed. The explosion, the boom, is terrible, atomic. The walls tremble. The lamp swings on its chain. There's no doubt what's finally happened. Will starts to cry, and I pick him up. "It's OK, it's OK," I tell us.

The first thing I see when I bring Will out onto that stoop of the river River Inn is a pair of sandals. They're formed to someone else's feet, but they're pointing out. My chest heaves with grief and gratitude, and my throat tightens with tears. It's eerie silent outside. The birds are silent, the trees are. I swear the river is, and the sky is a crazy, end-of-the-world, violet bruise.

I think: I hope he was there. I hope he was in that house. I hope the lava flowed over him, and stilled his body, and his arms, and his voice. I hope it buried him.

Now, it begins to snow. Gray snow, falling. Ash-like snowflakes. I let out a breath, an exhale. I want to sob with horror and relief and awe. I tilt my head up toward the sky. I watch the snow coming down. It's almost beautiful.

Inside that pine walled room, with its cigarette-burned dresser, and flowered bedspread kicked to the floor, the phone rings. It rings and rings until I reach it.

"He's been calling," my brother says. "Calling everyone." I remember those headlights. It's like he's back from the dead, but of course, he was never dead.

Five hundred and twenty tons of ash is darkening the horizon, steadily moving across the whole country. The waters of Spirit Lake boil, and the river thunders with mud, and trees are incinerated. Rubble, wreckage, anything once living is singed and sizzling. The damage will last for years and years. The damage will last through the generations.

But that mountain. It's still here, isn't it? There's a giant hole where it blew, but it's here. Sometimes, nothing wrecks the thing that destroys everything else. It alone will shake the ashes from itself and go on. It will stay and stay and stay standing, only now we understand what it's capable of.

In those sandals, I carry the baby to the truck, to find someplace where the sky isn't black. Harmony, Spirit, those beautiful words — they're gone. But Will is still here in my arms.

 Deb Caletti is the award-winning and critically acclaimed author of nearly 20 books for adults and young adults, including *Honey, Baby, Sweetheart,* a finalist for the National Book Award; *A Heart in a Body in the World,* a Michael L. Printz Honor Book; *Girl, Unframed*; and *One Great Lie.* Her books have also won the Josette Frank Award for Fiction, the Washington State Book Award, and numerous other awards and honors, and she was a finalist for the PEN USA Award. She lives with her family in Seattle.

The Department
of Long-term Catastrophes

Eli Francovich

Hugh Hubert, the proprietor, founder and sole employee of Hubert & Sons Long-term Catastrophes, sat at a grimy table and tried not to smile. He asked, "Have you considered volcano insurance?"

The client, a spindly, dark-haired man named Jake, shook his head.

The two men sat in a bland, damp room on the second floor of a strip mall in Kalama, Washington, along the banks of I-5 and within a stone's throw of the turgid Columbia River. It was a balmy 65-degree January day. The accumulated ice from a cold snap two days prior had nearly melted, its legacy water pooled along the town's main drag.

"It's a new bundle we offer," Hubert said. "Packages a lot of the traditional catastrophic business coverage into a bulletproof deal. Flood. Earthquake. Projectile damage, you name it. We call it the Johnston Guarantee."

Hubert had made the 35-minute drive from Portland earlier that morning. It was a beautiful day, the sky a brilliant blue and the sun warm. Although the northern horizon was hazy, steam-ejected ash lingering from last week's mini-eruption, the news said.

Jake owned a small business, transferring ancient VR memories to the newest bioformat, or something like that – Hubert couldn't remember – and had called him a few weeks ago struggling timidly to tell his story.

71

He needn't have wasted the effort. Hubert had heard it a hundred times. Probably even thousands. I used to just have regular, normal insurance. Seemed to work fine, but now, I don't know. I feel like nothing is covered … blah blah.

In Jake's case, it was a series of floods last spring, followed shortly by a deep freeze. The water, pooled up to a foot deep on the floor of his shop, froze solid. The insurance agency, "God bless 'em," only paid out half, claiming most of the damage came from the ice, not the flood and, after all, Jake hadn't purchased the ice-storm coverage.

Now, Jake was visibly nervous. His leg bouncing up and down like a rodeo clown. He was worried about his husband and daughter, he said. Hubert nodded along.

"But, I mean," Jake said, "how likely is a volcano?"

Hubert suppressed a carnal victory smile, instead leaning back in the chair and interlacing his fingers behind his head, letting his gut erupt over his belt in celebration of an imminent deal.

"Have you seen the news?" he asked. "The scientists think Mount St. Helens could blow any day now."

Later, as Hubert sat in the backseat of his car, navigating Portland's rush-hour traffic, he felt a tinge of guilt. The volcano package, for Jake at least, was probably unnecessary, although technically defensible. Kalama, after all, wasn't more than 50 miles from the mountain. And, with the 90th anniversary of its last big eruption nearing, the probability of another blowup was rising, although most experts agreed it was still a decade or more away.

And, Hubert guessed, Jake wouldn't be in business for another five years. In his decades working insurance, he'd developed a sense for a business in a death spiral.

He shook the guilt away; he'd rather not dwell on it. That was the nature of his business, and it treated him well. Catastrophes, of all kinds, were a growth industry.

Sure, he did the normal stuff. Floods, burglary and fire. But he'd managed to find his niche early on. Climate change and its harem of horrors. Artificial intelligence, job displacement, too. Meteor strikes, even.

With the discovery of other sentient life two years ago (they'd been sending Earth messages for nearly 100 years, but for various, inane and complicated reasons, NASA had been interpreting the signals as reruns of "Friends"), Hubert was in the process of drafting a policy covering an interstellar war and/or subjection. He might even draft a separate policy for extraterrestrial job displacement. He took a mental note to check and see what the competition was doing in that sphere.

Things changed faster than anyone could track. Technology, of course. But also, topography. Seattle had calved into the sea in 2040, when Hubert was 20. The weather shifted year to year. All this change, Hubert learned, made everyone very, very afraid. When in a philosophical mood, he believed people didn't actually fear death or financial ruin so much as chaos.

Insurance, even in the topsy-turvy world of the 2070s, remained a bulwark against mayhem. He believed that without a tinge of doubt.

His car arrived and parked itself in the garage. The lights flickered on, and the door opened. The house greeted him, asked him about his day, informed him dinner would be ready in 20 minutes and that it had successfully killed three mice. Was that a note of pride?

Tremors had knocked a few knickknacks off the mantle. He noticed and put them back; a picture of Mom and Dad. His brother.

He sat in the living room and checked his statistics. Slightly elevated heart rate. Above average water consumption. Below average caloric intake. Stable cortisol levels. His M.D. Assistant shipped the day's data to his insurance company.

The silence was oppressive, and he felt some dark mood coming on. Sensing this, the house put on music (an individually tailored mix of melancholy and upbeat pop designed to honor his internal state while slowly lightening the mood). He adjusted his dopamine levels, welcoming the familiar luminosity, a gentle aloofness that softened the worries and stresses of the day.

He rested here for some time, but his mind, impervious to the comfort of the situation, wouldn't let go of something Jake had said.

They'd been saying their goodbyes. Jake had put up an admirable show of pretending he would think it through, even though they both knew he was terrified and would happily pay for any modicum of peace of mind.

"I'll let you know soon," Jake said.

"No rush," Hubert replied while glancing at the water-stained carpet. "Hopefully, it will be a mild spring."

Jake looked miserable. The room smelled awful. Damp and old. It wasn't even hooked up to the internet. Hubert started out the door.

"It must be nice to own a business with your sons," Jake said.

Hubert stopped, his hand resting on the door frame.

"Yeah," he said. "Talk to you soon, Jake."

Wynonna had been gone for five years, but he still sometimes heard her voice in the home they'd shared. He'd barely touched her office; it had, over the years, become a shrine to their love. Anything and everything that reminded him of her he'd moved into that room, slowly filling it.

He didn't enter it much.

They'd met during a career retraining program. He was 32 at the time. His first career had just ended (he'd worked for Apple in tech support before they folded), and she was the course teacher.

He'd never in his life felt any strong sense – good or bad – about the rightness of things. In his experience, people who talked like that were usually woo-woo wackos who'd willingly forgo dopamine boosters in order to get closer to "reality."

He had no time for that. And yet, when he saw her that first day in downtown Portland, he was overcome by a deep knowing that they were meant to be.

That had been foreign, terrifying, exhilarating and completely irrational territory. He was smitten. And as they became closer, all the evidence supported his initial feeling. They fit; she balanced out his cynicism. Her job, after all, dealt in hope. And his caustic view of life provided an edge, he liked to think at least, that helped her connect with the desperate people cycling through her classrooms.

She later said she hadn't felt a similar "knowing," but it didn't seem to matter. Their lives seamlessly interlocked, and within six months they'd moved in together, a decision his friends warned against. But it went well. For 13 years, they'd had an ideal partnership.

And then she'd become pregnant.

He still remembers that day viscerally and completely. He was in Alaska trying to sell crop insurance (Sure, it's too cold now, but just look at the models. This will be the freaking breadbasket of the world in 20 years, brother. Think about your children.) when he got the call.

He'd called her back as soon as the meeting was over. Before the video even popped up, he could tell something was wrong. She sounded tense and tight – a cable stretched too far.

"I'm pregnant."

He almost laughed. That was impossible, right?

Apparently not.

Only later did he learn that the male pill, while nearly perfectly effective, was not infallible. He couldn't believe it. They had people living on the moon, and the Mars mission was about to launch, and yet the pill still failed? It strengthened his resolve to avoid space travel at all costs.

Adding to the seeming impossibility of the entire thing was the fact that Wynonna was 48 years old. On the flight back from Alaska, he'd figured out the rough probability of getting pregnant under those conditions. Statistically speaking, they'd won the freaking lottery (he even started drafting an Unexpected Pregnancy, Despite Best Efforts insurance plan, but the potential market was just too small to make it pencil out).

That night, they'd met at their favorite restaurant and then walked along the Willamette River.

"What are we going to do?" she'd asked.

Despite the shock of the day, he'd felt happy. The pregnancy made sense. Their relationship felt ordained, a crazy word to be using, and yet how he felt! He told her this shyly. She started crying. They hugged. He cried, discretely. They were going to be parents.

"Twin boys," the doctor intoned, examining the black-and-white, and oddly antique looking, ultrasound.

"Holy crap," she said.

"Holy crap," he said.

They made preparations. In a fit of exuberance, he renamed his business. She laughed and said he was sweet. Australia burned and desperate people arrived in boats and planes up and down the Pacific Coast. The insurance business boomed.

Then one day in early May, Wynonna, who still worked for the government helping people retrain for new careers, came home from work ashen. It had been a tough day. A class full of folks in their 70s trying to get jobs in biotech. Some were refugees from the East Coast. They smelled of desperation, she said.

"Want a dopamine shot?" he asked.

She shook her head no.

"Hugh, I've been thinking," she paused. Looked out the window. Fear gnawed at his belly, and he upped his dopamine level. He felt at peace and calm ready for whatever she would say next. "I don't think we should have these babies."

The words cut despite his elevated happiness index.

"Seeing those people in my class today, I just don't feel right about having a kid, and especially not two of them," she said. "Everything is so bad right now. Can you imagine what it will be like when they're 70?"

She couldn't imagine bringing a kid, let alone two of them, into this mess.

She was crying. He was crying.

They went back and forth. She wanted it to be their decision, she said, and he believed her, but of course the biological reality of it made it her decision more than his, didn't it? And her logic was bulletproof, he admitted, and so at the end, they made the rational choice.

They still loved each other, and they were committed to each other, they said. The pregnancy didn't change that, they said.

But, of course, it did. The fault lines widened. He searched in vain for some insurance against that, something that could hem them back together. And, he didn't change the name of his company, saying at first that it was more hassle than it was worth and soon saying nothing at all.

Jake called the next day.

"I've been thinking it over, and I'd like to add the volcano package," he said. "I did some reading last night, and, whoa, I had no idea volcanoes were so dangerous. That one in the 1900s or whenever, that was insane. I saw some of the photos."

Twenty minutes later, it was done. Hubert was a little wealthier, and Jake felt more secure. Still, after he got off the phone, that same, dark empty mood overcame him, and he felt none of the normal post-deal surge of power and accomplishment. Perhaps he was getting too old for this, he thought. He prepared for the day's meetings.

He was dressing, trying not to think too much, when a tremor raced through the house, the floor suddenly fluid. He stumbled and steadied himself on the dresser. He heard a crash from Wyonna's office, and the house started squawking at him. Another tremor shook the world.

"Seek shelter, seek shelter."

More crashes from the room, he tried to run but was tossed into the wall, nearly lost his footing but didn't fall.

The house yelled at him. "Volcano warning. Ash, earthquakes expected. Seek shelter, Hubert."

The floor settled, for a moment, and he lunged toward her office door, opening it and bracing himself in its frame. Another shock rocked the house.

Already, her room was a disarrayed disaster. The photos of her and him smashed on the floor, and her workstation toppled. A box full of her clothes broken open, its contents tossed about like driftwood.

The tremors stopped. The ground, so fluid a moment ago, returned to its normal solidity.

He stood there on the edge of the wrecked room and felt himself unraveling. He roughly wiped away the tears welling in his eyes and turned his mind to work and his back to the room. He didn't know the extent of the volcanic damage, of course, but, based on back-of-the-envelope math, he'd owe a lot of people a lot of money if he didn't get creative.

 Eli Francovich is a writer and journalist for *The Spokesman-Review*. His fiction has appeared in *Marry a Monster: Lilac City Fairy Tales Vol. II* and previously in Summer Stories. He is writing a book about wolves in the American West, one of the few places in the world where a resurgent carnivore population is coming into regular contact with a landscape dominated by humans.

Feast, Smudge, Snag: A Lakota Woman's Search for Everything Across Kohl's, Target and Barnes & Noble

Tiffany Midge

1. Feast

As a contemporary, urban Indigenous woman who visits the outlet shops and the suburban malls for all of her hunting and gathering needs, it's important to always give a blessing of gratitude to the designers, manufacturers and salespeople who gave their lives so I could shop at this JC Penney and purchase this 70% off pashmina scarf. And it's important to pay respects to the pashmina's spirit by tearing the receipt from the clerk's hand, stuffing it into my mouth and consuming its raw, potent and wild power.

2. Smudge

A few years ago, my office manager at work, Janet, handed me a copy of "Eat, Pray, Love." "It changed my life!" she said breathlessly as if she'd just climbed 10 flights of stairs to Enlightenment. "Elizabeth Gilbert is a Shaman."

Ouch. "Uh, OK," I said. "I'll check it out. Thanks."

"Oh, you simply must. It was so spiritual. I just know you'd appreciate it," Janet said.

Calm down, Janet. "Yeah? You know I'm not ... you know, spiritual, per se, right?

"Well, I just thought because you – um …"

"… Love to read?"

Janet looked relieved to be off the hook. "Yes, because you love to read! And reading is such a contemplative, and like, spiritual activity."

Could this interaction be any more awkward?

"Well, cool, thanks for the book." And just like that, the topic is closed. I don't have the time or energy to disabuse every non-Native person of their box of favorite cultural stereotypes. A few years ago, however, I would have dutifully climbed atop my designated lectern and delivered my standard TED Talk on contemporary, urban Indigenous people, but after a thousand times or more of being the Native version of Julia Sugarbaker, I'm done. I'm tired. Who has the bandwidth?

More often when these kinds of interactions occur – and trust me when I say they occur with alarming frequency, I could set my watch to them – I just let it slide. Or do my best to try and let it slide. Except for later, of course, the interaction will come flooding back, and I won't be able to fall asleep because I will be replaying the details back in my head. The conversation I should have had, the things I should have said.

3. Snag

The Klickitat story tells of Loowit, a beautiful young woman who Creator transformed into a volcanic mountain because she couldn't choose between the two brothers who fought over her. Their love triangle resulted in the creation of the Cascade Range we know of today: Mount St. Helens, or Loowit, and the warring brothers, Mount Adams, Pahto, and Mount Hood, Wy'east.

Like Loowit, my own romantic narrative, my origin story, is not without its faults, its eruptions, its fissures and, yes, its love triangles.

I learned about love from my mother and from her mother before her. Several Native women in my family married white men. All the way back to French fur trappers, so the joke goes. Auntie

Rondelle married a man who was literally so white even other white people teased him for being so white. And when Rondelle went to the grocery store dragging her tow-headed Village of the Damned children through the aisles, people assumed she was the babysitter. So, if the Creator took issue with Native women marrying white men, or visa versa, it could explain any number of seismological calamities, any number of meteoric disasters.

When Rondelle was a teenager, before she got married to the whitest man in the history of the world, she claimed Mount St. Helens erupted the morning after she lost her virginity, the implication being that losing her virginity was a moral failing, and surely God was steamed about it.

Mom said not to pay any attention to her. "God doesn't dole out punishments to people who are simply acting out their natural impulses." Which doesn't explain why Creator, the Great Spirit, was punitive and transformed Loowit and the two brothers into mountains. Or even why that origin story is so heteronormative, not to mention monogamist.

I always asked, "Why was Loowit expected to choose, anyway? Couldn't she have them both?"

4. Feast

I am descended from the Hunkpapa, of the Oceti Sakowin, but I grew up far from my reservation. I couldn't tell you what medicines to gather for which ceremony with the exception of sweetgrass or sage; and I couldn't tell you where timpsila – the prairie turnips – grow on those lands where my mother was born, and her parents before her, and so on, but, I like to think that one day, if I have a daughter of my own, that should she arouse a dormant volcano by losing her virginity like Auntie Rondelle, or incite a competition between two hot brothers for her affections, I will throw a feast in her honor. One day.

5. Smudge

I've been asking myself important questions lately, the hard questions, questions about lifestyle management and incorporating health wellness branding into my social media and daily routine. Questions like, how can I live my most authentic self? What is my life's purpose? Am I a living manifestation of joy? Is "Live, Laugh, Love" the right manifesto to use as an inspirational centerpiece in my dining room?

6. Snag

When people ask how Shayne and I met, I used to say it was at church, that our mutual requirement for piety and virtue had brought us together. I told people that Shayne passed me the offering basket where he'd just tendered travel-sized bottles of lotion. I told people that after the service, during the coffee and tea afterparty, Shayne came up to me while I was checking my messages and asked if I was texting with Jesus.

But the truth is I hardly ever went to church. The truth is I met Shayne at a Barnes & Noble author event. Literature is my church. The truth is it was during a rainstorm that seemed like a hurricane, and we were the only two in the audience. The author was Meskwaki or Cherokee or Shoshone or some combination thereof, and his book was about postcolonial grief and intergenerational trauma, a memoir about a memoir about a memoir.

During the Q&A, the other member of our two-person audience, Shayne, who I soon learned was from Tulalip, asked the author why so many Native American books are about trauma. He said he didn't mean to trivialize Native history and atrocity, but at the same time it seemed like books by and about Native Americans were mostly about fatality.

"Is the publishing industry only interested in trauma porn? Only interested in tragedy and redemption stories?" Shayne asked. "What about intergenerational joy? Intergenerational creativity? Intergenerational humor?"

I had been thinking along the same lines – intergenerational sarcasm, intergenerational whimsy, intergenerational weirdness. Could I even claim being Native if I didn't have a personal trauma narrative replete with a strong message of hope and redemption?

The Cree or Navajo or Kickapoo or Kiowa author weathered Shayne's questions with a slick professionalism. Shayne seemed very earnest, even humble, not at all like he was trying to bust the guy's chops, which I suspected he was. And even though there were only the three of us gathered at the corner end of the store, next to the maps and stationery, next to the remainder bins and wall calendars, I still felt a tension taking up the space, wanting to take root, but that might only have been the rainstorm pounding against the large panes of glass. It felt romantic and a little bit dangerous.

7. Feast

"Uh-oh, Grandma's making that soup again, try and be appreciative!" Grandma used to pack the ingredients in her suitcase and travel across three states by train just to make it for us when she visited. It was a winter stew she called washtucna, made from dried timpsila, dried bison or venison (really sawdusty) and dried corn. Reconstituted in the soup pot, the ingredients really left a lot to be desired. For my trashed palate, it tasted like rubber bands and toenails. Although today, I would give anything to have Grandma at the stove and making her soup. To sit with her in the kitchen listening to her talk about her life, laughing and teasing with us. But back then, as a teen, I had no idea. My identity as a Native had more to do with using every part of the sacred Dairy Queen dipped cone than timpsila.

8. Smudge

Thoughts that keep me awake at night: You know, Janet, I feel it necessary to clarify something to you, and that is that "shaman" is culturally appropriative, and in case you aren't aware, using that term comes off as an epithet.

I mean it's insulting to compare a white woman author to a "shaman." Why? Well, it's disrespectful to tribal people, particularly because you have no realistic notion or understanding of what a shaman actually is.

In addition, I feel it's necessary to point out that your wrongful assumption that Natives somehow corner the market on spirituality – well, see, Janet, that's a stereotype, it's essentializing, and these kinds of assumptions are based on fatally false brush strokes, which contribute to the preconstructed, prefabricated, shrink-wrapped, Leanin' Tree, fantasy Indian paint-by-number chicanery set that the white supremacist narrative insists on dishing out and chugging down.

Yeah. That's what I would have said, if my official Indian Authority Card from the Office of Pissed Off Natives hadn't expired.

Eventually, I did get around to reading the bestselling memoir "Eat, Pray, Love," and later I saw the movie starring Julia Roberts, and while I couldn't altogether relate to Elizabeth's midlife crisis, I could relate to her search for wholeness and self-fulfillment. I might not have been a white woman of wealth and privilege residing in the upper echelons of East Coast society, but I knew a thing or two about a broken heart. I knew a thing or two about pasta.

9. Snag

On our first official date, Shayne took me to a photography exhibit of natural disasters. When we came upon the collection of Mount St. Helens photographs, I told him that I was conceived the night before it erupted. I told him that my mother had been a virgin, that she was only 15, that she didn't know the man, my father, that he still remained a mystery. I confessed that my family lied to me most of my life, that my actual aunt raised me as her daughter.

"Is that TMI?" I asked.

"What's TMI? Is that like a UTI?"

"Yes, Shayne, it's exactly like a UTI. I'm infecting you with more information than you might care to know."

"That's impossible."

"Why?"

"Because I want to know everything there is to know about you. And how you came to be in the world is pretty danged important."

I felt a large balloon of expectation and longing collapse in my chest as if Shayne had just yanked the rip cord of my heart, and I was free-falling into his depths.

 Tiffany Midge is a citizen of the Standing Rock Sioux Nation and was raised by wolves in the Pacific Northwest. She is the recipient of Submittable's 2020 Eliza So Fellowship, a 2019 Pushcart Prize, the Kenyon Review Earthworks Indigenous Poetry Prize, a Western Heritage Award and the Diane Decorah Memorial Poetry Award and was awarded a 2019 Simons Public Humanities fellowship. She is a former humor columnist for *Indian Country Today* and the author of *Bury My Heart at Chuck E. Cheese's* (Bison Books), which was selected for the 2020 Spokane Is Reading program.

Red Zone

Ben Goldfarb

Hank went down to the dock before dawn. Dirty spring snow lingered along the cobble path that led from cabin to lakeshore. The mist hung so thick that he heard the canoe before he saw it, the rhythmic clunk of aluminum on wood. He flipped the bowline off its cleat, knelt on the damp timbers, grabbed the gunwales and lowered himself into the boat, which rocked and then settled. The dew that soaked the aft seat crept through his jeans. He pushed off the dock with the wooden paddle and the canoe spun away, its snout pointing toward the glassy heart of Spirit Lake, a compass needle to true north.

The fishing tackle lay where he'd left it, in the muddy bilge water on the canoe's floor. Rod, tacklebox, carton of nightcrawlers dug up from the woodpile. Hank threaded a crawler onto his hook and flung the rig. The bobber vanished into the mist, landed with a distant plop. Hank leaned forward, the rod light in his fingers, the canoe adrift.

His canoe. His dock. His cabin. He hadn't yet gotten used to the pronoun. The place had been theirs, though Hank's own ties to the cabin ran deeper than Mark or Rebecca could fathom. They loved the place in their own shallow way but were not of it. Not the way Hank was. The sealant that bound its logs practically ran through his veins. His father had laid the final cedar-shake shingles on the steeply pitched roof in 1950, or so his mother told him – the year Hank was born. He'd never lived in a world without it.

Whether the world would let him have it, though, was another matter.

Two years of legal wrangling had finally concluded that winter – the dispute resolved in Hank's favor, as he'd known it would be. The deed to the cabin had arrived in a manila envelope in late March, liberated from the purgatory of a lawyer's filing cabinet. Hank gazed at the document reverently, held it to the dingy light that seeped into his cramped kitchen in Kelso. He touched his mother's signature, faint and spidery. She'd struggled to hold a pen by the end.

The mountain stirred that week as though in response to this seismic development, smudging the crisp blue sky with a mile-high tower of steam and ash. Hank watched the footage, awed but unworried. The mountain had backdropped much of his life, and he'd seen it in all its moods: flame-lit at sunrise, engulfed by cloud, bone white in spring, slate-colored by fall. Nothing it did could surprise him.

But humans were more reactionary than mountains, and by the time he drove up in early April – the deed folded in his glove compartment, months of canned food in the bed of his F-100 – the Red Zone had been established. Near the mountain, the road to Spirit Lake became a crime scene, choked with hasty concrete barriers and signs that read "Hazard Area." A Forest Service cop lowered his razor-burned face to Hank's driver-side window. "You got a permit?"

"I got a place on the lake," Hank said.

"You still need a permit," the ranger said. "Scientists and law enforcement only. Governor's orders came down last week."

Hank stared. "For some steam?"

"Gonna be more than steam, brother."

"Doubt that," Hank said. He slapped the steering wheel and turned the truck back the way he'd come. He drove slowly this time, scouring the roadside wall of Doug fir, and after a few miles found what he sought, an overgrown logging track knifed into the timber. He glanced into the rearview to make sure no one was on his tail, then swung onto the old Weyerhaeuser road, leaving asphalt behind.

He stashed the truck behind an alder thicket, loaded his Army-issued rucksack with supplies – plenty of food at the cabin, but who knew how long this inanity would last – and set out. Hank hiked through clearcuts and stands flagged for harvest, waded streams swollen with frigid melt. He'd come up on a Sunday, and the woods were empty of loggers. He reached the cabin by sunset, just as the last pink blush of day lit the wispy steam billowing from the mountain's summit.

Hank got his first bite after 20 minutes on the lake. He reeled in the rainbow, slit its throat and slipped the stringer through its gills. The fish bobbed alongside the canoe. The mist was burning off, and he could see the mountain now, its profile distorted by the tumorous bulge that had grown near its summit, staving in its peak like the dent in a fedora.

For weeks the mountain had been restive, disgorging black columns of ash that roiled like midsummer thunderheads and flashed with lightning. Once he swore he'd seen a blue flame flickering above its crater, eerie and alive. At night the cabin shook, tin camping plates and mugs clattering like false teeth in the cabinets. But the volcano had gone silent for a couple of days now, and Hank suspected the show was over.

Hank appreciated the mountain's histrionics: the frequent flyovers notwithstanding, it kept the lake quiet. The Spirit Lake of Hank's childhood had been utter cacophony – the growl of outboard motors, the screams of waterskiers, the braying laughter of men grilling hot dogs. Mark and Rebecca had contributed to the din. They'd been a high-spirited, rowdy pair, always cannonballing off docks and banging screen doors and jostling for prime marshmallow-roasting position. Hank, nearly a decade younger than his siblings, spent summer days alone, excluded from their canoe races and wrestling matches by dint of his youth.

By the time he was 10, they'd both slid from his life – Mark to college and then law school in New York, Rebecca to California to do, well, something. His father was long dead by then, too. Hank vaguely recalled a towering, genial presence, redolent of gin and sawdust, placing a kind hand on his shoulder.

Through it all, the cabin remained – snug, solid, stubbornly well-crafted. Every June, Hank and his mom left Kelso the day school let out, trunk loaded with groceries and board games. They spent summers in the mountain's protective shadow, fishing off the dock by day and reading by firelight at night in companionable silence. Her energy had waned since her husband's death, but that suited Hank fine. When she went upstairs to lie down in the afternoon, he split wood or searched for elk sign. At school, Hank was a solemn, inscrutable shadow; the cabin, without his raucous siblings, offered a refuge where no social stigma adhered to solitude. Where the only cohabitant, his mother, seemed to require as much personal space as he did.

His eyes on the bobber, Hank briefly tried to compute the date. He'd kept count for a couple weeks, then lost track in late April. Now it was mid-May, he was almost certain. The 16th, maybe. Or, no – the 19th. Not that it mattered. He had nowhere to be, no dependents and an infinite supply of fresh fish.

From the silence, he knew the Red Zone was still in place. He'd decided against using the fireplace, which made for cold nights, but Hank suspected that he'd catch crap if anyone saw smoke curling from the chimney. He wasn't sure if the authorities could force him out, but he had no desire to deal with a fresh-faced Smokey Bear-type imploring him to save himself. The cabin had only just become his, and you couldn't pry him out with a crowbar.

Yesterday morning, he'd thought briefly that the blockade had lifted. He'd been reading on the couch – Conrad, an eternal favorite – when he heard engines, doors slamming, male voices. Sharp knuckles rapped on the sturdy pine door. Official knuckles.

"Anyone in there?"

Hank held his breath, eased back into the couch. He heard two sets of boots shuffling on the porch, muffled voices, the words "evacuation" and "unoccupied." The door rattled against the thrown deadbolt. The boots thumped away.

When the men were gone, Hank crept upstairs, raised his binoculars to the bedroom window and peeked out. Up and down the lake, his neighbors bustled from cars to cabins, cabins to cars, loading cardboard boxes into trunks and backseats. He deduced the situation: The governor, still laboring under the delusion that the mountain was dangerous, had suspended the Red Zone to let homeowners collect their belongings. Sheer idiocy, Hank thought – if the mountain really was at risk of erupting, why let folks in at all?

All day, he watched people he'd known since childhood prep for a catastrophe that would never come. There was Andy Ailey, owner of the most decrepit powerboat on Spirit Lake, tossing duffel bags into his Olds. There was Lisa Webster, whom he'd once seen sunbathing topless, taking a smoke break after filling her Pontiac with trash bags of clothes. Through the binoculars, they seemed as tiny and inconsequential as termites, twitchy with aimless industry. He felt a sudden, crazy suspicion he'd see Mark and Rebecca among them, then remembered that his siblings had no claim here. Wherever they were, it wasn't Spirit Lake.

It was only natural that Hank, now a man, had gravitated again to the cabin in 1972. He'd tried living in Kelso after discharge, he had, but his stint in the jungle still hovered over him, somehow tugging his strings. Bar fights, lost jobs, a hazily remembered car crash. A night in jail, then two. "This right here is your one war hero pass," the sheriff told Hank the morning he let him out. "Don't think you'll get another."

Hank went to Spirit Lake to cool off for a few days. He stayed five years. In summer, he fished; fall he hunted elk; winter he plowed through 10-foot drifts in a snowmobile checking a trapline. Mark and Rebecca, who'd both ended up in Seattle after their wanderings, visited sometimes – his brother with a whiny pack of sunburn-prone kids, his sister in the company of a smug conscientious objector. No one had anything to say to him. Hank grew a beard. Other families along the lake, who'd known him as an odd but gentle child, nodded politely and avoided chitchat when they ran into him buying beer at the general store. When he needed conversation, he sought out Harry, the profane old guy at the lodge who'd pour whiskey and Cokes and swap war stories. Harry bobbing in the Atlantic after his troop transporter was drilled by a U-boat; Hank hunkering in the jungle as ragged lightning lit up Khe Sanh.

And he had his mother, of course. She came up often to read on the porch, stick her toes in the lake, watch the mountain change color with twilight. She was a secretary at a dentist's office now, and it occurred to Hank that she'd started working again so that she'd have an excuse to go back to Kelso each Sunday evening to escape the dolorous man her boy had become. When they read together by the fire, he often looked up from "Lord Jim" to find her watching him, flickering shadows etched in the deep crevices of her face.

Still, when she'd gotten sick in '77 and refused hospitals and hospice, there was no question who would assume her care. Hank boarded up the cabin and moved back to Kelso to spend the next year by her bedside. Mark and Rebecca flitted in and out, dropping off flowers and fruit baskets; it was Hank who peeled the oranges and fed her the segments. It was Hank who read Austen aloud to her, who held her papery hand, who brushed her lank hair and threw away the clumps.

Hank brought up the cabin in the final weeks of her life. He'd gathered from conversation with Mark, her executor, that joint ownership would fall to all three siblings – an arrangement he found intolerable. Let his brother and sister have the money, the Kelso house, whatever jewelry hadn't been pawned. The cabin meant nothing to them and everything to him. Hank, with her bedside as his bully pulpit, had convinced his mother of this wisdom and persuaded her to hire a lawyer to change the will – or, more accurately, let the lawyer that Hank found change it. Three weeks after she signed the new document, she was gone.

The legal proceedings began a month after her death. Mark and Rebecca, wielding the phrase "undue influence" like a battering ram, argued that their scheming younger brother had manipulated a senile woman. Hank's attorney, hired out of the yellow pages with some G.I. savings, pointed out that their mother had been nail-sharp to the end. Why, she'd completed the Sunday crossword two days before she died.

His siblings fumed to no avail. Hank knew they would never speak again, that the narrative of the devious brother who'd seized the family home would become enshrined in their own histories, passed down through generations like a heritable disease. Decades from now, grandnieces and grandnephews he'd never meet would tell the story, their outrage still fresh. We had a summer house on Spirit Lake until some mean uncle stole it. Well, let them.

After two hours, Hank had caught four fish, enough to last a few days. The snow-filled couloirs that veined the mountain gleamed in the morning light. Spirit Lake spread before him like a mirrored plain. He guessed it was 7:30 a.m.

His thoughts wandered to his brother and sister: Mark teaching him to pierce the thick pale band at the nightcrawler's midsection so the trout couldn't nibble it off the hook; Rebecca pointing out the elk picking their way across the mountain's face. When the Red Zone ended, Hank decided with a burst of charity, he'd let them come to the cabin for a day or two. Give them a chance to sift through the photos and knickknacks that clotted the cupboards and shelves. Salvage a few keepsakes.

Hank bore them no ill will, he'd told them repeatedly – at mediation sessions, over the phone and finally in formal letters on his lawyer's stationery. They simply had no purchase here. They had their own lives; the Spirit Lake house was his. And he knew they'd been wrong about their mother's mental state – unlike them, he'd been there for her. She'd given him the house not because he'd manipulated her, but because she alone knew what it meant to him.

Hank spun the canoe toward the shore, toward the cabin with the pitched roof that squatted in the lakefront pines. From a distance, the place looked weathered and durable, sculpted more by nature than by man – a landscape feature as eternal as the forest or the mountain itself. It was his habitat, he thought, as surely as the bear's cave or the owl's tree hollow, and he'd been right to claim the only place he'd ever felt at peace. He had a sudden vision of himself as an old man rocking on the porch, ankle crossed over knee, the lake stretching before him to lap at the mountain's toe. Hank dipped his paddle and headed for home.

Ben Goldfarb of Spokane is the author of *Eager: The Surprising, Secret Life of Beavers and Why They Matter* (Chelsea Green Publishing), which won the 2019 PEN/E.O. Wilson Literary Science Writing Award. His journalism has appeared in the *Washington Post*, *High Country News* and the *Guardian* and his fiction has been featured in *Motherboard*, the *Bellevue Literary Review*, the *Allegheny Review* and the *Hopper*.

Bandits

Sharma Shields

When Mom fell in love with the man of ash, we tried, at first, to be happy for her. We vacuumed, we mopped, we sang. We swept up the ashes without complaint. Even then the thin film of him settled beneath our fingernails or whirled up at us from a plumped cushion, catching in our eyelashes. We muttered to each other as we combed him from our hair. We couldn't be rid of him even when we were alone.

We'd loved the man of light. He'd shuffled through our house gently with his long, glowing hair. If we wanted our space – and we always wanted our space – we could easily hide from him in the shadows. He didn't get all over us the way the man of ash did. But Mom felt very little for him, and then she felt nothing at all. He lived now in the downstairs broom closet, and it comforted us to know he was there, glowing alone in the darkness even if we never ventured there to check on him.

The man of ash was different: He paid us too much attention. I saw the way he watched Fern when her back was turned, his gray hooded eyes dark with hunger, his lips moving subtly within his shaggy charcoal beard. One day she passed too closely by him, and his dense, smoky arms unfurled and clasped her around the waist; he pulled her smoothly into his lap. For a moment, I couldn't see her; she was lost in the cloud of him. Nearby, Mom coughed.

I lifted from my chair and hurried to my sister, groping for her hand.

"Let's go outside," I said, my fingers encircling her wrist, breathing in the fumy deep smell of him.

He met my eyes, scowling, but to my relief, he released her. Fern rose mechanically from his gloom, her dress filthy now and cindered, and Mom issued a nervous laugh.

"Like scared horses, my girls," she'd apologized. "They're not used to men."

But we were used to men, all sorts of them, the man of light, the man of thunder, the man of air who flirted with Mom but stayed just out of her grasp. What we weren't used to was a man who wanted every part of us, who would smother and dirty and settle into us ruinously.

"If he touches you again," I told Fern once we were alone, "I'll murder him."

My tone frightened her. "Nothing's happened, Minnie," she argued. "I just got too close."

"It's not your fault, numbskull," I spat and regretted my tone when she flinched.

We grew careful then, edging along the walls, crawling near the baseboards. We threw buckets of water on the floor to try and sop up the ash that now carpeted our whole home, but it was futile. We retreated whenever we could to our bedroom or to the fresher air of the backyard and garden.

One day after we weeded the garden beds, as I lay on my sore back on the lawn, I told Fern we should run away.

My sister was always swift to argue with me, to call out my poor decisions. It wasn't the first time I'd suggested such an enterprise. She plopped down next to me on the grass, and I awaited a quarrel.

Instead, she laced her fingers through my own.

"This crystalline air," she said. "Good for the lungs."

She brought my hand to her mouth and kissed my knuckles in a goofy way, and I laughed. I was so grateful for this backyard, the garden we'd tended, the fresh air. The house was covered in his film now, the state of it worsening by the moment.

"We'll be bandits," I said. "We'll leave them behind."

Fern's smile flashed and then faded. "Why does she always choose them over us? What's wrong with us?"

"She'll never change. I know that now." Then I added, irritably, "Nothing's wrong with us, Fern."

Fern absently poked at a hole in her sneaker. "We'd be happy, just the three of us. Maybe one day, she'll see it."

For years, we'd done all we could to shake Mom out of her misery. We cooked, we cleaned, we gardened, we drew her bath, we ironed her clothes, we made the beds. But the drinking, the men, the poor choices continued.

"A bandit's life for me," I sang, shaking Fern's hand gently.

She sprawled out near me and put her head on my shoulder. "I hate everything," she said, as she sometimes did.

"But I love you," I rejoined. "Most of the time, anyway."

From the open window in the house came a protuberant cloud of ash, billowing, settling, edging cunningly toward us. Fern eyed it warily, and I eyed her.

"Minnie," she whispered, desperate now. "Tell me what it will be like, our bandit life."

We crept away from the house on hands and knees, toward the small orchard with its squat apple trees.

"We'll walk the railway all the way to the big lake," I said. We tucked ourselves behind the tree trunks, the tendrils of ash curling and uncurling, searching for us. "We'll cross the narrow bridge over the water and skirt the town.

"There will be an abandoned cabin in the trees not far from the river, and we'll break in through an unlocked window. It will be stuffy and dusty there, but no ash. We'll throw open the windows and doors, and we'll clean the entire place top to bottom until it glitters and gleams. It will be ours and ours alone."

"And Martha the Bear?"

"Of course, Martha the Bear is there, too."

"And Peter the Fox?"

We were too old now for stuffed animals. We were menstruating girls who in normal situations would soon start public high school, but I didn't – wouldn't – argue with her.

"Yes, Peter, too. From time to time, we'll steal into people's homes for food and supplies. We'll boil tea from dandelions and foxgloves. We'll braid columbine in our hair. In the summer, we'll bathe in the lakes, and in winter, we'll tend the fire in the woodstove."

"And Mom?"

"Eventually she'll come to live with us," I lied.

"How will she know where to find us?"

I shrugged. Just the idea of her coming for us at all had exhausted me. I wasn't sure she ever would or ever had.

The house was quiet. Soon, we knew, she would call to us to come inside, to hug her. She would force us to hug him, too.

"We leave," I said. "Or we choke."

Fern rested her chin on one knee, her gaze on the house. Her face was slightly broader than my own, friendlier, but one of her eyes was darker brown than the other so that she always seemed half in shadow. This was how people could tell us apart if they bothered.

"Minnie," she said. "Look."

I twisted around to see. The yard was filling up with ash, smothering our garden. We could see the tiny trails of dying insects as they wiggled and flailed against the invasion. From the murky rooms, we heard Mom's cough: hacking, now, violent; she'd absorbed too much of him. We pulled up our T-shirts over our noses, stepped across the powdery detritus, hurried to our room.

"Tonight," I told her, reaching into our closet to retrieve our bags. "Or else."

To my relief, Fern agreed.

Days passed, then months. In our dusky cabin near the big lake, we wiled away the hours. Men of stone, men of trees, men of water, men of ice, men of light and ash; none of them bothered us. Now it was just stone, trees, water, ice, light and the sparkling dust made from our own living bodies.

We no longer cleaned up daily but on Mondays, and that suited us fine. We took jobs at the local grocery, one of us with a shift in the morning and the other with a shift at night. In the summer, we put on our jewel-colored jelly sandals and walked into town. We bought Popsicles and perused books at the library. We knew disasters were unfolding both near and far, but we paid them no attention. We were free from anyone's terror but our own.

I was alone when Mom arrived. Fern was searching for fiddleheads in the woods; she wanted to make an omelet for supper. She was curious about a set of boys who we worked with at the grocery.

"They're not men of any one substance," she assured me, and she talked of inviting them over.

I didn't encourage or discourage her. After having a mother who didn't care enough, I didn't want to be a mother at all, only a sister, a friend.

It was Mom's cough I heard first.

The rattle of it rent the air; its vibrations skimmed across the lake.

I'd been staring out at the calm water over a sink-load of dishes daydreaming of summer and swimming. We wondered if and when the family would return to their summer cottage, which we'd broken into swiftly and easily not long after crossing the narrow bridge, and we feared the moment of arrival the way we had once feared God.

In a bedroom bureau, I'd found a red swimsuit, and it fit perfectly. I'd stood in front of the bureau's large mirror, and Fern, holding Martha the Bear on her lap, exclaimed that if it wasn't for the port-wine stain across my chest, I'd look like a supermodel. We'd laughed for an entire night about that, imagining a more glamorous life for me as a catwalk ingénue. A life of caviar and expensive clothing and rich friends and loneliness. The opposite of what we shared now.

And now that familiar cough. I stepped outside, still wiping my hands on a dishrag, and there she was, our mom, a long, pale specter emerging from the tall grass. I crossed the gravel carport to speak with her, but Fern was already there, putting her arms around mother, sobbing.

Oh no, I thought. Fern would invite her in; Fern would make a new home for her. And it would all begin again, all of the neglect and harm.

Mother coughed, and the ash sailed out from her lungs. The man of ash was inside her, she'd never be free of him, and she'd brought him to us like a disease.

I heard what she mumbled to Fern, that she was sorry, that she was a terrible mother, that she needed our help. Coughs erupted one after another, expunging dense scuds of volcanic rock and glass, and my sister, assailed by them, transformed into an old woman before my eyes, flesh and hair graying and singed.

To my chagrin, she embraced our mother even harder, telling her she was understood, she was seen, and I sank into a paralysis of misery. Fern would be destroyed by her own capacity for love. I'd always known it. I couldn't approach and free her — my feet held fast to the gravel as if I were a tree newly planted.

I prepared myself for the end of us.

But then Fern, squeezing Mom even tighter, tears staining her ashen cheeks, said, "I love you. But I can't let you near us now, Mom. For Minnie's sake. For my own."

The embrace intensified. Mom's cough worsened. Her eyes bulged, her bones cracked. Muscles and viscera liquified. Fern held her in such a tight embrace, her whole body rippling from the effort, that I worried the earth would open up beneath our feet, the sinkhole swallowing us all.

I called out Fern's name, to let go, to save herself, but my voice only strengthened her resolve. She bore down, and the embrace became a vise, then a spike, then a fire. The heat of it assailed us. All at once, I regained motion of my feet and stumbled forward, blindly grasping for my sister's shoulders.

The ash settled around us. The clouds, having gathered darkly overhead, released a cleansing rain. In Fern's hands, she held what was left of our mother, a small ceramic ring, which Fern offered to me, gasping.

"You wear it," I said. I was so grateful, so moved.

We stood in the afternoon light just the two of us, facing the water. Taking up her hand, my flesh grazed the threadlike circle near her knuckle, the small, firm proof of Mom's remaining love. The rain sluiced over us, returning my sister's youth to her, the gray melting from her hair in grotesque clumps. I was shocked at how strong she'd become, how resolute. I gave her hand a squeeze and then let go.

Before us, the lake was just lake. The stone was just stone. The light was just light. The boys my sister wanted to befriend were just boys. This was what I hoped, anyway. We allowed the day to yawn before us, as filled with potential for good and ill as any of us living beings.

I breathed deeply the petrichor. I hid my naked hands in my sleeves.

 Spokane writer Sharma Shields is the author of the Washington State Book Award-winning novel *The Sasquatch Hunter's Almanac* (Holt Paperbacks), the story collection *Favorite Monsters* (Autumn House Fiction) and the Pacific Northwest Book Award-winning novel *The Cassandra* (Henry Holt and Co.). She lives in Spokane with her family.

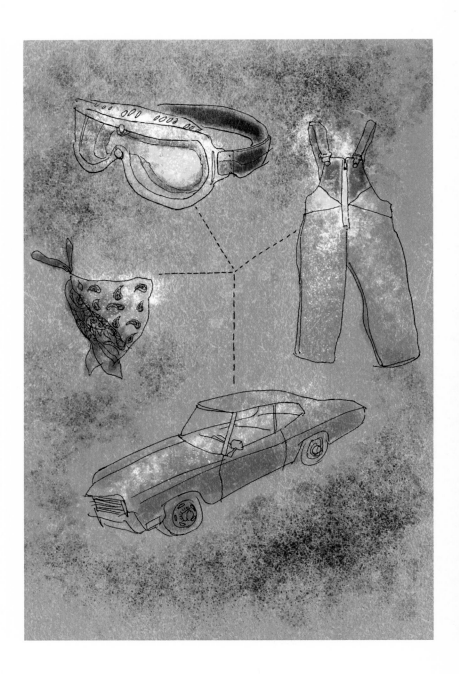

St. Helen and the Spokanites

Samuel Ligon

Paw Paw said it was just hippies on the mountain got smote. And fornicators. "Nary a Christian among them," he said.

"What about my grandpa Murphy's camp," I said.

"Closed," Paw-Paw said. "And they was Catholic anyway – not Christian."

"Catholic is Christian," my mother said. "And it's not just hippies up there."

"So blame your lesbian governor," Paw Paw said. "If that makes you feels better."

"Dad," my mother said.

"Lesbian?" I said.

"Everywhere," Mee Maw said, "with their pantsuits and raucous talk."

"Not like the good old days," Mom said, "when we were all miners and loggers and prostitutes."

"Prostitutes?" Garrett said, and Paw Paw said, "You don't know a thing about the good old days."

"Nor loggers," Mee Maw said. "Nor miners. But it used to be –"

"Indians," our mother said.

"And cowboys!" Garrett said.

"You don't know a thing about Indians," Paw Paw said, "nor migrant workers, nor any of the others you take up for."

"Nor sodomites," Mee Maw said. "Nor Israelites."

"They're just people up there," our mother said, "like anywhere else."

The light dimmed in the living room, the first sign of the cloud coming.

"And now His wrath is upon us," Paw Paw said.

Garret cried as the sky went darker. Our mother picked him up, even though he was too big to be picked up. "It not God's wrath," she said. "It's ash from the volcano."

"It's literal brimstone," Paw Paw said.

"Come here, Seth," my mother said, pulling me in with my brother. "It's going to be all right."

"You don't have to cry about it," Mee Maw said.

"He can cry if he wants to," my mother said.

"I'm not crying," I said.

Paw Paw had the radio blasting.

"You're lucky you got out when you did," he said. "Lucky you listened, for once."

We'd been in Spokane since the mountain woke up, but Mom said it wasn't about that.

It was about money.

"It was always in him," Paw Paw said.

"Don't," my mother said.

"To slink and slunk —"

"Leave it," Mee Maw said.

Lightning sparkled through the falling ash, prickling our necks and arms.

My mother wrapped us tighter.

"The top of the mountain appears to be gone," the radio said.

"Gone?" Garrett said, and Paw Paw said, "Good riddance to bad rubbish."

"Where did it go?" Garrett said.

"On top of us," Paw Paw said.

"Was Dad there?" I said, and my mom said, "Of course not."

"Could have been," Paw Paw said.

"Leave it," Mee Maw said.

"Likely as anywhere," Paw Paw said.

But I didn't believe him. The camp wasn't on top of the mountain anyway.

"Get in the car, boys," our mother said. "We're leaving."

I headed for the stairs and my stuff but didn't know if my old school would take me back.

"I don't want to go out there," Garrett said.

I turned and looked at my mother.

Her eyes were closed tight.

"You're not going anywhere," Paw Paw said.

Our dad had been gone a long time, but we stayed in Longview and waited. He used to take us to the abandoned camp on the mountain Grandpa Murphy had built, with its falling down cabins and pool full of dirt. We camped there before kindergarten, the next year, too. Mom said I couldn't remember all the times we camped there, but I did – Garrett pouring water into the lake, how it sparkled as it tumbled from his jug, Mom and Dad on the shore at night kissing.

"Sometimes you can't see the blessing for the sin," Paw Paw said.

I was under the card table where the train was laid out, our suitcases piled by the door. It was still snowing ash, but we weren't allowed out in it. Garrett was watching TV. Paw Paw had made the train and the tracks and the little people who could ride it, pioneers and Indians and outlaws, plus a tunnel from an old cracker can.

"Of course you did the right thing," Mee Maw said in the kitchen. "The only thing you could do. And this is where you are now."

"Just don't say he was there then."

I heard the clicking of Mee Maw's lighter.

"Nobody said that," Paw Paw said, and my mom said, "You said it."

"He could have been anywhere," Paw Paw said, "is what I was saying."

"Are you so mean," my mother said, "you don't understand your own words?"

"Don't think for a minute," Paw Paw said, "I won't throw you out again."

"Leonard," Mee Maw said.

I was ready to go.

"Constance," Mee Maw said.

Garrett didn't notice anything outside the TV.

"Come on now," Mee Maw. "Let it go for a minute."

"For the boys," she said. "For you, too."

"Is that what you'd do?"

"Can't you see it might be a good thing," Mee Maw said, "to let him go," and my mom said, "No. I can't."

"I'm not saying he was a bad man," Paw Paw said.

"Of course you are," Mom said. "You say it and you think it and you always have."

I looked at the people on the train waiting to be annihilated by Indians and outlaws.

Garret jumped off the couch and zoomed around the room, singing with the kids on TV.

Our dad might have been at the camp or he might have been anywhere in the world. The only places I ever thought of him were on the mountain or at our house in Longview, on the porch or feeding the wood stove or cooking with my mom at night. Never here with Paw Paw and Mee Maw. The hard part's not knowing, our mother always said. He could be in jail down in Mexico, she said. Or drowned in the Sound and washed out to sea. He could show up any moment, she used to say. But he never did.

Our dad said there was a spirit in the mountain and all around that place. "You can feel it," he said. "There's my father," he said. "There's Uncle George."

Mom and Garrett were still asleep. It was cold up there so early in the morning.

"Like a ghost?" I said.

"Kind of," Dad said.

"Like God?" I said.

Mee Maw and Paw Paw talked about God, but Dad never did.

"You can call it that if you want," he said.

"Do you call it that?"

He pulled the coffee pot from the fire and started mixing pancake batter.

"Get me those huckleberries," he said.

I opened the cooler, the bag leaking purple juice all the way back to the fire.

"Is that what you call it?" I said.

"I don't call it anything," he said. "It's more of a feeling."

He dropped the berries into the batter.

"How about some bacon," he said.

I went to the cooler and pulled out the bacon.

"Like a saint, maybe," I said.

"I don't know much about saints," my dad said, "to tell you the truth."

It got loud in the kitchen again, then quiet. Our mom came into the living room. "We're going," she said. Outside, the sky was full of ash. We had to bundle ourselves in winter coats and snow pants and goggles for protection. "Toxic ash," the radio called it.

"You'll never get anywhere," Paw Paw said. "The interstate's closed."

"Constance, please," Mee Maw said. "The boys."

"I don't want to go," Garrett said.

"Don't be a baby," I said.

"You're the baby," Garrett said.

"Let's go," our mother said, and we walked outside, the ash over everything, the sidewalk, the lawn, our Chevy Malibu parked in the driveway.

"Where are we going?" Garrett asked when we were inside the car.

"Home," our mother said.

He pulled off his hat and goggles and wriggled out of his snow pants.

We were covered in ash.

"I thought this was home now," he said.

"Hush, Garret," I said.

"You hush," he said. "You're not the boss of me."

Mom turned on the radio and turned it off.

Garrett didn't remember our dad.

You couldn't tell what time it was, just dark, all that ash sweeping and swirling. I had friends in Longview, but Mom said someone else was in our house now, another family.

I hardly remembered him, either. It had been over a year. Maybe two. I didn't know how long it had been.

"We'll stay with your cousins," Mom said. "Till we're back on our feet."

The car started bucking and coughing.

"No," our mother said.

We made it another block before the Malibu died completely.

"Goddammit," our mother said.

She tried to start it again.

"Goddammit," she said, pounding the steering wheel with her open hands.

A man knocked on her window. "Ain't going anywhere," he said. "Filter's clogged."

We sat for a minute while ash covered the windshield.

"It's OK, Mom," I said.

But she didn't try to hide her crying, which made Garrett cry in the seat behind us.

We bundled back up, Garrett sniffling. The streetlights were on, and more people were outside. Everything felt upside down, night in the afternoon, a snow day in summer, all of us bundled and covered in that soft, light ash. You couldn't help sticking out your tongue to try to catch some. It tasted like pennies, or like water from the lake, just a little on your lips when you came up for air.

There were markings in the ash for days, like on the moon or in the mud by the lake. If you followed those lines, you'd find a dead bug, a bee or a grasshopper, covered in ash. Sometimes there were animal tracks, dog or cat, wolf or badger. I gathered ash, filling jars with it. Everyone did. Moose tracks appeared, bear and cougar and sasquatch and other animals big enough to survive. I imagined them pulling themselves from the ash on the mountain and making their way to Mee Maw and Paw Paw's patio out back, hundreds of miles from home.

The rest of the mountain would come to Spokane, too, Mee Maw said, but only if I believed it would, only if I prayed hard enough to make it true. The ash became sludge when Paw Paw tried to wash it off with a hose. Someday, our mother said, everything would be just like it had been. But that wasn't true, either. And the rest of the mountain stayed where it was.

 Samuel Ligon is the author of the novels *Among the Dead and Dreaming* (Leap Frog Press) and *Safe in Heaven Dead* (Harper Perennial) and the story collections *Wonderland* (Lost Horse Press) and *Drift and Swerve* (Autumn House Press). A co-creator and co-editor of *Pie & Whiskey: Writers Under the Influence of Butter and Booze*, Ligon teaches in the creative writing graduate program at Eastern Washington University and is artistic director of the Port Townsend Writers' Conference.

Hope

Dan Gemeinhart

As a matter of fact, I never wanted to kill my neighbor's cat. But sometimes things happen, and sometimes one thing leads to another, and sometimes you're just kind of swept along in a landslide, and then all of a sudden you're trying to hide a dead cat. It happens.

It all started like three days ago, when the ash started falling.

I'd just blown up at my mom. The explosion was a long time coming, I guess. Building up inside me, hot. If she coulda seen me, I bet my face woulda been white and splotchy like it gets when I'm mad. My eyes lightning bolts.

But she couldn't see me, of course. She never can. Not unless they invent a telephone that lets you see who you're talking to, and that ain't likely. When she told me she wasn't coming to see me, again, I just erupted.

"Of course you ain't!" I shouted. "You never do! You ain't come to see me since you left!" Which is true, as a matter of fact. She's always promising to come and visit, but she never does and she never has, not in the three months since she walked out. I just got tired of it, I guess. I yelled some other words that ain't generally considered polite and then hung up hard enough that my hand kinda hurt.

I ain't never yelled at Mom before. Never hung up on her, neither. But, heck. Sometimes when something's pent up for too long, it comes out hot and loud. And then, watch out.

Dad hollered from the bedroom, "Hey! What was that all about? That ain't no way for a 10-year-old girl to talk!"

"None of your business!" I shouted back. "And as a matter of fact, I'm 11!"

Dad thought about that for a second. I knew he was scowling, like he always does when it's pointed out that he ain't that smart, which is pretty often.

"Well," he said sulkily, "It ain't no way for any kid to talk."

I glared at the ashtray, sitting there on the kitchen table next to the phone. I won't let Dad get rid of it, even though he don't smoke. Mom's the smoker, and someday she's coming back. I made it myself, in school, fired in the kiln and everything. It's kinda lumpy and wobbly, a crooked circle covered with what's supposed to be polka dots but really just look like stains. It's empty now, but before she left it always made me proud to look and see it full of ash and butts. When I think of her, it's that burnt smell of cigarettes that's strongest in my mind and the sound of her singing. I hated it back then. But I miss it now.

"You OK?" Dad called. He knew who I'd been talking to.

"Just peachy," I answered, then slammed out the back door onto our deck. "Deck" is probably a generous term. Our trailer is only a single-wide, but it's setting at the top of a slope, so Dad and his brothers built a deck off the back of it. It's pretty close to sturdy. I stomped out and leaned over the rail. Ten feet below was the yard and the round, domed lid of our barbecue. Past that, a bunch of bushes and trees and then the Spokane River, gliding along quiet.

It was so cloudy, it was almost dark, which was weird 'cause it'd been sunny all morning.

"Ten years old," I muttered, then spit and watched it drop down to the ground.

Dad is a piece of work, and sometimes work is the nicest word I'd use to finish that description. He was too young when they had me, everyone says that. He does his best, everyone says that, too. Maybe it's just that his best ain't all that great. But, heck. Maybe him being a dad is like me doing fractions. We gotta get some credit just for showing up.

I hear footsteps creak up behind me and I know it's dad, showing up.

"She ain't coming, huh?" he says, and I just spit again. "Maybe she'll make it next weekend."

I just snort and rub at my eyes.

"Yeah. Probably not. But you can hope, I guess."

Hope. Shoot.

"Hope is the thing with feathers," I say.

"What?"

I shrug.

"It's something Carole said." Carole's our neighbor. She thinks she's some sort of an artist, but I think she's some sort of a weirdo. "It's from a poem, I think. By some lady."

"Huh," Dad says, and I agree. Carole said it like it was all meaningful or something, and I kinda smiled but really I was like, *I don't know, that sounds pretty darn vague.* Still, the words got kinda stuck inside me.

"Well. Don't get all crabby about it." And then he goes back inside. Jesus.

He means well, I guess, but I ain't taking advice from a guy who can finish three cans of Rainier during one episode of "M.A.S.H."

It seemed like it was getting darker and darker. My eyes were burning.

I looked at the birds sitting in the trees. Mom loved the birds. We got two feeders, nailed to the deck railing, but they were both empty as the ashtray inside. It's like everywhere I looked, I saw the emptiness Mom left behind.

Then, it started to fall. I blinked, trying to make sense of it. Little floating bits of white and gray. Saw some land on my sleeve. I bent to look, but my breath blew 'em away. More fell, though, and then more.

Soon, it was everywhere. Dad came out with me, and we watched it fall. Ash. Ash, ash, everywhere. We turned on the radio and heard about that volcano, way over there. The birds were still and silent in the trees, the goldfinches flashing bright like gold dust in muddy water.

"We probably shouldn't be breathing this," Dad said, but we both still stood there and watched.

"What'll the birds eat?" I asked.

"Whatever they normally do," Dad shrugged. "It's just ash. Their food ain't going nowhere."

But I frowned. Looked at the feeders. Empty in a gray world. Why would something pretty as a goldfinch ever come back to an empty feeder?

I went to the garage and I found mom's big tub of bird seed, and I filled up the feeder.

Mom called again that night. But I wouldn't talk to her.

School was canceled 'cause of the ash. As a matter of fact, school being canceled ain't all that fun when you can't go outside and you ain't got an Atari. Who'd've thought we'd ever get stuck at home, schools closed, and have to wear a mask to go to the store?

So I spent most of my days watching the birds coming back to the feeder, singing their songs. Puffs of ash when they landed on a branch. We left the ash on the back deck. I didn't let Dad sweep it off like most people did. I liked how it looked like snow. I could see my footprints from when I refilled the feeders. And the tiny three-toed tracks of the birds where they landed. I could see where things left from and where they came back to. I liked it.

It was on the second day I found the dead goldfinch. Lying on the deck. Bright and still. I thought the ash had killed it, somehow. But then I saw 'em, over on the stairs leading down to the yard. Paw prints, in the ash. Leading straight over to Carole's house.

"Ginger," I hissed, glaring at the prints. Ginger is orange and white, with green eyes and a swishing tail.

The next day, I found two more. A chickadee, black and white and precious, and another goldfinch. The birds were wary now, watching the feeders from the trees but staying away.

When Mom called that night, Dad talked to her for a long time. But I wouldn't take the phone. I was still red hot.

On the third morning, I found another body, lifeless in the ash. A little white and brown thing, eyes closed.

And then, that afternoon. Slouched at the table. Back door standing open to let in a breeze. Going crazy from being locked all alone for three days. My hurt boiling up inside me. Rumbling. A couple birds were braving the feeders.

Then, Ginger. Creeping up quiet, behind the empty flowerpots. Paws silent on the ash. Eyes electric. I sat up. She got right under the feeder, looking up. I jumped to my feet at the same time she leapt up at the feeder, claws spread wide to snare a thing with feathers.

I didn't waste any time thinking. My anger exploding out of me. Ginger landed on the deck rail, a goldfinch struggling in her claws. I grabbed that crappy clay ashtray off the table and roared and chucked it through the door, hard as I could.

Ginger flashed her head to me at the last second, ears back. The ashtray thunked off her skull and her body crumpled, limp. She tumbled over the rail and out of sight. The loud, echoing dong of her hitting something.

I stood there, frozen.

"Crap," I whispered. I waited for the sound of her running away. But there was silence. I tiptoed out and peeked over the deck's edge.

There was Ginger. Still as a statue. A cloud of ash swirling in the air around her.

They say cats always land on their feet. As a matter of fact, sometimes they land on their back on a barbecue. And stay there, apparently.

I gulped and ran down and approached her slow. But I knew. She wasn't breathing. And her back wasn't in the shape you'd hope to see if you were rooting for her to live.

Nine lives my foot. I suppose there were two or three ways Ginger might've died in that fall, though, so I guess she'd already spent six or seven by the time she went after that bird.

I sighed, looking at her twisted corpse. It was a heckuva throw, but I wasn't proud of killing her. Now there'd be an empty dish at Carole's house, an empty spot on the windowsill. That's what happens when things blow up, I guess. They leave quiet, and emptiness, and ash.

I buried her out under the trees. Had to carry her down there under my shirt in case Carole was looking. It was gross. She was still warm.

I looked down at the little mound covering her up, down by the water. Thought of the birds, unburied.

"Rest in peace, murderer," I said.

Back on the deck, I scraped the ash off the slats with my feet, erasing Ginger's tracks. Refilled the bird feeders. My little eruption had killed. But it had cleared the way. The birds could come back. Maybe that's also what happens when things blow up. They make room for a return.

I could hear Dad talking inside. On the phone.

"Yeah, they're saying, like, 50 dead or something. Quite a deal."

Fifty-one, I thought, counting cats.

"Well, anyway," he says. "This weekend. You promise? Like, you really promise?"

I hold my breath.

Something flutters in my heart. It's a new thing.

"OK. I'll see you then."

My eyes burn, and it ain't from the ash. The thing inside me stretches its wings. It's gold, and fragile, this thing inside me. It's got feathers, I think.

As a matter of fact, it might be hope.

Dan Gemeinhart is the author of five books for younger readers, the most recent being *The Remarkable Journey of Coyote Sunrise* (2019, Henry Holt). Gemeinhart is a Gonzaga University graduate who worked for 13 years as an elementary school librarian and teacher. He lives in Cashmere with his family.

Ashes to Ashes

Julia Sweeney

It was a Sunday morning in May, and Ben had just left Angela's dilapidated Seattle apartment building in good spirits. After a year of flirting, yearning and maneuvering (and with the aid of some Jack Daniels added to the espresso they sipped while playing chess at Last Exit on Brooklyn the night before), he'd finally gotten Angela to invite him home. A stupefying soup of oxytocin, dopamine and seratonin swirled through his veins.

He could hardly control his face from smiling as he closed the apartment building door behind him. Wisteria blooms hung from above the entryway to the otherwise neglected courtyard, and the scent was powerful. Even his vision seemed keener. On the sidewalk, he looked up to her second-floor window. She stood there, looking down on him, wearing her *Quadrophenia* tank top, her dark, long hair cascading majestically around her muscular shoulders. Juliet looking down on Romeo. The sun, shining right into her window, obscured her face, and Ben put a hand to his forehead to shade the bright rays. Maybe more like Moses looking up at Yahweh.

He mimed tipping his hat to her with a slight comic bow – "Thank you, M'Lady." He couldn't tell if she could see him. Maybe that was weird. Maybe he shouldn't have done that. She was older than him – 27 to his 20; he would have to watch out not to appear ridiculous. He grimaced and looked away, silly – too silly? That had happened, too, the night before. A joke she'd made. He wasn't quite sure if she were laughing with him or at him. How comfortable was he being teased?

He guessed he would have to accept that kind of thing, being with a clever woman who is seven years older.

He turned and looked across the street at his '68 VW bug, the passenger door held on by an orange bungee cord. Mary Kate. She'd done that. Mary Kate was Ben's high school girlfriend back in Spokane. He tried to teach her how to drive a stick, and she'd landed them in a ditch. They both laughed so hard they waited several minutes before getting out to survey the damage. Then they laughed even harder. Now that was funny.

But that was three years ago. Now he was a college man who lived in Seattle, and he was seeing an older woman. He liked the sound of that. I'm seeing an older woman. My girlfriend is older than me. It sounded titillating. Older woman implied sexual expertise. Nice. But was she his girlfriend? No, but she could be. Couldn't she? Was she? He felt he could make it happen. Couldn't he?

He swerved away from this uncomfortable uncertainty and let himself feel the full onslaught of the thrill of success. Yes! He remembered being on a roller coaster some years back, that sensation in your body as you come off that first climb and descend to earth, only to see a bigger hill ahead. Giddy. That was the word.

Ben and Angela both worked at the Varsity Theater in the U district, a block or so from the University of Washington where Ben was a junior studying astronomy. He sold popcorn and tickets; she ran the projector upstairs. The theater played indie films, and they played for a long time. *Quadrophenia* had run for eight months, then they began playing a German film by Rainer Werner Fassbender, *The Marriage of Maria Braun*. (When Ben looked back on this time, which he often did, he began to see that the transition from *Quadrophenia* to *Marriage of Maria Braun* tracked his own concerns. Rock 'n' roll mayhem giving way to the desire to couple up and hunker down. The Who to whom.)

Ben was attracted to Angela from the moment he met her. Her demeanor, even the way she moved, demanded a certain privacy. She exuded a kind of solitary, unaccompanied essence that hung in the air around her like Pigpen and his dust cloud. Only not smelly. In fact, the opposite.

Ben was generally gregarious and chatty. He liked to connect to people. Certainly, the other guys at the dorm weren't spending all their time figuring out how to worm their way into the mind of a girl like Angela. No one understood his attraction to Mary Kate in high school, either. She, too, was a step off from the rhythm of her peers, a mostly solitary person. Her piety and quiet nature made her come off as imperious at times, but Ben could see through it to her sincerity. Mary Kate's high school nickname had been Mother Superior. It'd been hard for Ben not to tease Mary Kate back then when they'd finally connected physically – those powerful, awkward early collisions – and sing to her "Mother Superior jumped the gun." Mary Kate would absolutely not have laughed at that one.

It occurred to Ben that both Angela and Mary Kate were loners and that maybe he had a type. And what was Mary Kate doing right now? Was she really joining a convent like she'd said in her last letter? Was he the only guy who didn't realize she'd always been committed to a much more important guy, that guy in the sky? Was his rival God? Why did sleeping with Angela open the door to thoughts about Mary Kate, lurking in the wings of his awareness? It was as if she was always ready to bound onto center stage.

Maybe it was because he could still feel Angela's body under his fingers. And it made him feel a vague lingering guilt, like he had betrayed Mary Kate. Even though he had not! Absolutely had not! They were unambiguously not together anymore.

Ben glanced at his hands gripping the steering wheel as he drove south. They looked remarkably like his dad's hands, which seemed creepy to notice in this moment, his dad burrowing his way into his sexual encounters. Ben noticed that he had the same callus on his forefinger and the split fingernail on his ring finger. It must have come from all that working with dough at the doughnut shop, and certainly not from counting the dough, which was meager and hard won. His dad had owned and personally run the Donut Parade, a modest coffee shop up on Hamilton and Illinois. He became known for his maple bars. The family lived a couple of blocks away.

Angela's body, athletic and muscular, was nothing like Mary Kate's, who was curvy and soft. Angela's body also held surprises. She had a tattoo of Mount Rainier on her back. Mount Rainier! What kind of girl had a tattoo of Mount Rainier? Angela said, "In 20 years time, tattoos will be ubiquitous, especially on women." Who said 20 years time? And ubiquitous? What was she, British? No, she'd told him, she was from the Upper Peninsula of Michigan. In the small wee hours, as they lay together spooning, his head resting on her back, in the snow at the summit of Mount Rainier, she'd told him some of her story.

Ben tried to remember. She had, for the first time, become somewhat chatty, just as the exhaustion of the evening was gallivanting through his body calling him to sleep. Angela had had a difficult time at home growing up. Her mother had a string of alcoholic, explosive boyfriends. Things got bad. She considered ending her life. She stopped talking to anyone about anything. One day she passed a used-book shop with a box out front. For a dollar, she picked up "A Year in Paradise" about some Shmoe living for a year, in 1920, on Mount Rainier with his wife. The book catapulted her out of her world. She decided to get a tattoo of Mount Rainier on her back. She knew a tattoo artist. She would do it. The mountain's enduring, unchanging permanence answered deep needs. She literally wanted Mount Rainier to have her back. And of course, then she had a new mission: to move to the Pacific Northwest.

She'd met a guy while still in Michigan, Dave, a few years older, and an actual geologist. He was studying the volcanic rock that rimmed the Upper Peninsula, and she had been wandering around the scrappy woodland near her house. They dated on and off for several years. He was in Seattle, too, working at Mount St. Helens waiting for the expected eruption. He had done geological work on Mount Augustine in Alaska. "My grade school was named St. Augustine's," Ben thought but fortunately did not say. It would've been the kind of comment that would've betrayed how sloppily he was listening to her.

And anyway, Ben didn't like to think about this guy, this older guy who was an actual scientist and not flunking out of astronomy at UW like he was. Ben concentrated on the part of the story where they weren't seeing each other anymore. When Ben learned her ex had been a volcanologist, he imagined him Spock-like with pointy ears. But as he slipped his jeans back on in the morning, he saw a picture, and he was blond. Huh. So, they both had blond exes.

Angela was funny. When he sheepishly explained he was flunking his optics class, she said, "Well, that's not gonna look good." And when he'd said he thought she was shy because of her difficult past, she said, "Hey, there's only room for one projectionist in this room." Clever. You had to be on your toes with her, alert. It made him feel honored that she'd let him in and made him feel uncomfortable in ways he didn't entirely understand.

Ben stopped at the light at 50th and University. It was remarkably clear, like Seattle was previewing summer, and had sent the rain clouds offstage. People had an extra energy, seemed more alert. Green was bursting through everywhere.

As he waited for the light to change, Ben wondered if he should invite Angela to come with him this summer to Loon Lake, where his parents had a cabin. He imagined what it would be like to present his family with this attractive older woman with a tattoo on her back (of Mount Rainier!) as his girlfriend. He could see his sisters in their bikinis and his mother in her flowery skirted suit and his father in his knee-length trunks. And Angela coming out of the cabin, towel draped off her hand, walking into the water, turning, and yes, they would see it. His sisters would think it was cool, his mother would make some awkward comment, and his dad would say nothing. Dad was quiet because he was that sort. But, there was another reason he'd be quiet.

His dad was dead. It was hard to keep remembering that. His dad had died only a year before. It was remarkable how loud his father had become now that he was dead.

Mary Kate was Ben's only official girlfriend. She took Catholicism quite seriously unlike most of the other students who moved easily between the cultural Catholicism of the school and the modern world. She was open about her convictions, and so she was especially hard to court. Fortunately, she wasn't an evangelist. Or a scold. They'd met at Gonzaga Prep, junior year, the first year the school admitted girls. Mary Kate's former high school, Holy Names, had just closed its doors. She lived with her aunt a few blocks from school. Her parents were wheat farmers on the Palouse an hour south. Ben and Mary Kate had driven down together one Saturday in the late summer, the wheat stalks brimming and bowing supplication under the sun. They stopped at Steptoe Butte and climbed to the top and yelled out "Amber waves of grain!" to the yellow-gold world around them. They tried to summon the wind so they could catch the waves. Just after that was when he tried to teach her to drive, and Mary Kate promptly wrecked the car. He'd never had a strong desire to fix that door, and now he drove around Seattle with Mary Kate's orange bungee cord around the passenger door. A talisman of their union.

Ben saw Mary Kate's bedroom at her parents' farm. Cut-out images of saints adorned the walls like they were movie stars. The crown molding staged multiple Infants of Prague, like some sort of celestial orphanage for royalty. Where many girls had posters of Ryan O'Neal in their bedrooms, Mary Kate had hung one of Pope Paul VI proudly above her desk. Her eccentric devotion appealed to Ben.

In their senior year, up at Loon Lake, Mary Kate was helping Ben close up the cabin for the winter. After consuming a stale loaf of bread and a bottle of red wine (Ben did not make a joke about the body and blood of Christ), things went farther than either of them expected. The next week, Mary Kate explained patiently to him, and with admirable resolve, that while she was glad it happened, it wouldn't happen again. And, if she were pregnant, she would have the baby. He'd figured. A few anxious weeks of sweet misery followed. If they had to marry, he wouldn't have been able to go to college. He'd just learned he had gotten a scholarship to the University of Washington.

If they married, he would've had to start working full time with his dad at the Donut Parade.

It's true, Ben suddenly thought, that if that had happened, he would've been there for the last two years of his dad's life as the cancer came back again and again. He felt a pang of ... what? Equal parts relief and regret. The family understood. After all, he was off becoming an astronomer.

Except he wasn't becoming an astronomer. He was failing out of his program. It was the math that got him. He liked looking at the stars at night, naming the constellations, thinking about how small we were. But it turned out the field of astronomy was seriously about math, and Ben was not very good at that. He'd just failed two of the three required math classes. Multivariable calculus didn't have a variable that allowed for incomprehension. The scholarship was going to end when his GPA was revealed. Ben didn't know if he wanted to recommit and retake the math classes. Why didn't someone tell him astronomers spent all their time on graphs, databases, following algorithms? He'd lost his interest when he understood what the day-to-day life of an astronomer would be like.

Ben got close to the theater and began to look for a parking space, which he knew would be easy since it was Sunday. The first matinee was at 2 p.m. In *The Marriage of Maria Braun*, the title role is played by Hanna Schygulla, who reminded Ben of Mary Kate, strongly and unnervingly: her wheat-colored locks, her pointed nose, the comfortable nature with which she held her body, especially how she moved her hands. But mostly it was the tenor of her voice.

The first time Ben was invited up to the projection booth, when Angela had asked him if he could bring her some popcorn, he'd been struck by the darkness. It seemed fitting that Angela would have a job where she could work with most of the lights off. The carbon-arc projectors were ancient, and the clicking sound of the film's sprockets created an eerie soundscape that mirrored his beating heart. At one point, when they were whispering, in mid conversation, Angela took a cigarette out of her pack, opened the side panel on the projector and lit it off the arc lamp, her eyes on Ben the entire time. He involuntarily gulped; she was astonishingly beautiful and in command. The word "erotic" floated across his prefrontal cortex. Yes, that's the word. Erotic. Ben thought for a second he might literally swoon. That would have been a disaster.

And then be recalled his high school English teacher, Mr. O'Connor, who had a thick working-class Boston accent. While guiding the seniors through a section of the book *Dangerous Liaisons*, he described a passage as "erotic." At first, many in the class thought he'd said "erratic." It became a recurring bit among his friends, "That film was so very erratic." "He wrote both poetry and erratic literature." "I'm into erratica."

Remembering this worked. As he beheld Angela, standing there at the projector with her cigarette, half her face lit up and the other half shadowed, he didn't blush, or perspire visibly, or break the intensity of the moment with chatter. He took it in in its fullness, and he stored away this image like a secret gift just for him. From behind Angela's head, through the small square opening for the projector lens, Ben could see the movie screen in the auditorium. Hanna Schygulla was jumping up on some old gymnastic parallel bars in a boozy club where her character, Maria, is applying for a job. She says, "You might not need anyone apart from me." That line was a cue to Angela to prepare the next reel, and she shifted her gaze from Ben to the other projector, readying it for the transfer.

"You might not need anyone apart from me." Ugh. Ben wanted Mary Kate to leave him alone. How long would this movie play at this theater? Was Mary Kate trying to send him a message through Hanna Schygulla? Absurd. However, he had gotten that letter from her, which he hadn't answered, telling him that she was going to enter a convent after graduating from Gonzaga University. One might ask why Ben was looking for messages cryptically sent to him through Hanna Schygulla when Mary Kate was sending him actual messages.

Ben drove past the theater and saw a parking spot across from the street right next to the University Book Store. As he pulled into his space, he realized that people on the sidewalk were looking up in the sky to the south. Getting out of his car, he looked in the same direction.

Mount Rainier had smoke swirling around its top, like a meager brown toupee. An older guy on the sidewalk, looking in the same direction, said, "It's Mount St. Helens. She finally blew."

"Oh. Wow," Ben replied and stood there, transfixed by the billowing ash. Rainier stood right in front of St. Helens, like one actor upstaging another.

The man continued, "Did you feel the earthquake this morning?"

"No," Ben replied, becoming mesmerized by the site of smoke thundering into the sky.

"Yeah, not many people did. 8:30 a.m. I guess that's what finally opened her up."

Ben tried to remember more of what Angela had told him about her ex, Dave, and wondered if he were up at the mountain, and if the phone ringing that morning, which she'd ignored, was from him. Ben grimaced, understanding that he hadn't paid enough attention. He sighed and looked at the sidewalk. What did he really even know about her?

When he raised his eyes again, heavenward, he could see the smoke and ash were blowing east even while much of it still hung in the air cradling Rainier like a cloud of unknowing.

In their senior year religion class, Mary Kate and Ben read an anonymous 14th century mystical classic, "The Cloud of Unknowing." The basic idea was that one should not spend time thinking about God's particular attributes or actions, but the way one can truly know God is to surrender your mind and ego to an "unknowing" and thereby possibly glimpse, or feel, or thrill to the true mysterious nature of the Almighty. Mary Kate had been deeply moved by it; Ben had seen it as another way for the church to dodge scrutiny and avoid critical thoughts about God's existence. They had argued, he'd made jokes about it. Maybe too many jokes. Sometimes, Ben thought, admonishing himself, he didn't know when to be quiet. Mary Kate found his reaction to the text disturbing and revealing. This turned out to be the beginning of the end. She couldn't be with someone who didn't at least, on some level, respect her religious devotion. And Ben couldn't fake the kind of faith she admired. So, she had gone off to Gonzaga University to study theology, and he had gone off to the University of Washington to look heavenward in his own way.

Ben couldn't move from his spot on the sidewalk – more and more people were stopping and looking south and into the sky. He realized he was trembling. Even though he knew the lava was not headed toward him, the image of the eruption was deeply disturbing. He felt afraid, even terrified. The sensation of fright came from somewhere deep inside him, like an automatic fear of snakes, buried in ancient generations only to reveal itself now. A part of him was thinking how silly it was that he was shaking and scared, but another part was enveloped in the terror and in utter awe at the destructive power of the earth, of nature, of mountains. Adrenaline surged through his veins, overtaking the dopamine and serotonin and leaving him with his heart beating loudly, so loudly he wondered if others could hear it. He took a deep, slow breath trying to calm himself. And then this chattering voice inside him, this justifying explaining part of his neocortex, took over and wouldn't stop talking.

Ben understood, in some slim way, that his mind was creating a "deliberative experience" for him. "The rational choice show" was being played by the projectionist in his head, and he went through all the reasons, thoughtfully and seriously, the pros and the cons, a debate performance where everyone knows the decision has been made already.

Ben understood he was quitting college and moving back to Spokane.

There were so many good reasons to go home. For example, the ash would certainly be heading toward Spokane. Who knew what havoc it would create for his mother and sisters at the Donut Parade?

He would try to win back solid, unmovable Mary Kate, too. He would explain to Angela that his family needed him back home. He would be kind. She would understand. He would pack up his dorm, he would quit his job at the Varsity, and he would say goodbye to his roommate, and he could do all this in a couple of days. He knew he would try to call his mother as soon as he got into the theater. What if they closed the roads? There was so much to do. Ben's mind became quite busy.

Forty years later, on the anniversary of the eruption, in the wee hours of the morning, Ben was making dough for doughnuts. More than ever did he understand the Cloud of Unknowing. Which was kind of funny because over the years, he and Mary Kate had switched positions, theologically. She had become a religious skeptic, and he gave himself over to the idea that most things were mysteriously pre-arranged. Mary Kate figured it was because he was bad at math. But anyway, they hardly ever argued about it.

Ben had a telescope on the roof of the shop, and when he came to work early enough, he would spend a few minutes looking at the sky.

Julia Sweeney is an actress, monologist and writer. Her books include the memoirs *God Said, 'Ha!'* (Bantam) and *If It's Not One Thing, It's Your Mother* (Simon and Schuster). She spent four years in the cast of *Saturday Night Live*, and her film credits include *It's Pat, Pulp Fiction, Stuart Little* and *Monsters University*. She has recently been seen in the Hulu series *Shrill* and Showtime's *Work in Progress*. Look for her in the forthcoming third season of Starz's *American Gods*. Sweeney was born and raised in Spokane and now lives in Los Angeles with her family.

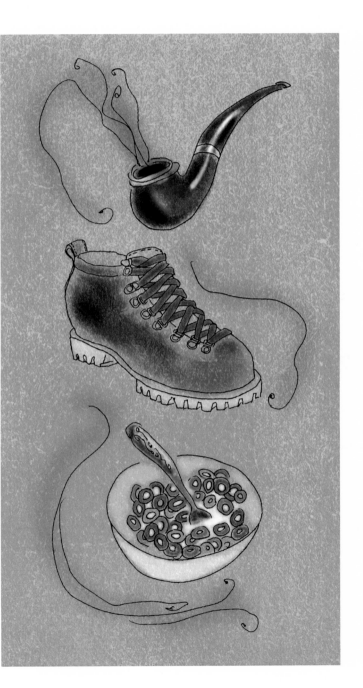

What Rises Beneath

Jess Walter

It was quiet for 140 years. Then, in March, the mountain began to rumble: earthquakes, bursts of steam, blue flame, ash clouds that sparked 2-mile bolts of lightning. All spring, the volcano seethed, spewed and shuddered, magma bubbling up its throat and pushing the north flank out 5 feet a day.

Five feet. Like a new human being every day.

That's what happened to us, too. On April 24, 1980, my sister Tanya and I found out a new human being was joining our family.

"Wait," Tanya said. "What?"

"You're having a baby?" I stared at Mom's flat stomach.

"No." Mom took a deep breath. "You have a 12-year-old brother. Patrick. He's coming to live with us."

Tanya and I stared at each other.

"But Tony is 12," Tanya said.

This was a good point. I was 12. Tanya was 15.

"Wait," Tanya said, "Tony has a twin?"

"No, Tony does not have a –" Mom's face went red, and she muffled a swear word. "You know what. I'm gonna let him explain it himself." Then she stormed out of the room trailing blue flame and 2-mile bolts of lightning.

The "him" was my dad. He was a chemist who worked for a grass and seed company, and when he got home from work that afternoon, he took off his wire-rimmed glasses and sat sweating in front of my sister and me.

"Several years ago," he said, "your mother and I were having difficulties. This was right before we found out your mother was pregnant with Tony, and we reconciled. Now occasionally when adults have difficulties, they seek out the comfort of … well … other adults."

"Oh, God," Tanya said.

Dad cleared his throat and looked at me. "Tony, I'm trying to remember how far you and I got in our discussion of procreation last month."

I held up my left hand in an OK sign, took my right index finger and put it through the circle, simulating …

"Right," he said. "That far."

"I'm going to puke now," Tanya said and went to her bedroom.

My dad and I stared at each other.

It was quiet for 140 years.

"Is he taller than me?" I asked, finally.

He wasn't. He didn't even make it to the shoulder of the social worker who brought him to our house that night. He reminded me of a feral cat with an unruly thicket of black hair and nervous, dark eyes. He had a jagged mix of baby teeth and permanent ones, like a shark's mouth. He arrived with only the clothes on his back: Oshkosh jeans, moon boots, gray T-shirt.

He wouldn't let go of the social worker's hand.

Mom made up the sofa bed in the basement, then went through my old clothes and made a pile for him.

That's what got me. Seeing this … creature … wearing my clothes. I'd wake up every morning and go to the kitchen for breakfast, and there would be Patrick eating the last bowl of Froot Loops in my old jeans and my white Ocean Pacific T-shirt. The one with the surfer on it.

"That's my favorite shirt!" I objected.

"You haven't worn that shirt in a year," Mom said.

"Yeah, because it's so special!"

Patrick wore the shirt every other day. He loved it. And my old Mattel handheld Basketball I game, which Mom had also given him.

I got Basketball II for Christmas, so technically I didn't play the old one much, but still.

"But still!" I said to Mom.

"Tony, I know this is hard," she said. "It's an adjustment for all of us. We all have to make sacrifices."

From what I could see, the only one making sacrifices was me.

Tanya mostly ignored the basement creature. When she did notice him, it was with the look you'd give a slug that crawled up and suddenly started speaking Spanish. What? And gross.

Mom fed and clothed the creature, took him to the doctor and dentist. And the creature liked her the most. He met her eyes and actually talked to her. The rest of us, he'd mumble, Mmm-hmm, if he meant yes, Mmm-mmm, if he meant no. But he'd look up shyly at Mom and say, almost in a whisper, "Can I have more green beans?"

The creature was stealing my mom.

Dad, too. He took Patrick for a haircut, and, on Saturday, took him for walks. I knew all about those walks because he used to take me. In between puffs of his pipe, he'd ask about school or tell me about sick stuff like procreation. He'd also point out science-y things like crabgrass in the Baileys' lawn or how fruit trees pollinated.

They were the most boring walks ever.

And now, I missed them! Mom could tell I was upset because she spoke quietly to Dad, and the next Saturday he showed up in my bedroom doorway with his pipe in his teeth. "Feel like a walk, Champ?"

"Mmm-mmm," I said and went back to playing Basketball II.

When you're a kid, your family is the basic underlying equation of the whole world, a physical and mathematical constant: two (2) adults + two (2) kids = 1 family (subset: house, garage, dog [hit by car, replaced by dog with same name]) – father home from work at 5:15 p.m., dinner on the table at 6, visit grandparents every other Sunday, presents opened Christmas Day (duh).

It had been this way since the dawn of time, you figure, the bedrock upon which the earth was built.

What you don't know is what rises beneath that bedrock. That your father has been out procreating with strangers, sticking his index finger in their OK signs. That your mother will rifle through your best things and give them to some basement creature. That your parents will one day bring home a replacement for you. The world is shattered. What permanence? What normality? The world is fragile, random, dangerous.

At school, Patrick was a grade behind me, in sixth grade while I was in seventh. So that meant he was still in elementary school, and I was in junior high. That was good, although we still had to take the bus together.

This was how the last straw happened.

It was early May, and we were walking to the bus stop together, Patrick a few feet behind me. It had just rained, and I looked back to see he was stepping in mud and looking down at the pattern the soles of his shoes made. Just like I used to do.

I looked at his shoes.

My old waffle stompers.

The creature was stomping mud waffles in my favorite shoes!

Sure, they were small now, but I still loved them. Not liked. Loved!

And no one had asked if the creature could have them.

I stopped. Stared at the shoes. Last straw.

Superheroes aren't the only ones with origin stories.

Supervillains have them, too. And this was mine.

"Give 'em to me," I said.

Without a word, Patrick sat down in the mud, untied the shoes and handed them to me. He walked to the bus stop that way, got on the bus, went to school and eventually came home. I assumed he went about his whole day in wet, squishy socks. And I was glad.

Two weeks later, Mount St. Helens erupted: 57 people killed, 250 homes destroyed, 47 bridges and 185 miles of highway. The entire north side of the mountain collapsed, dissolving into the lake beneath it, the largest landslide in recorded history, followed by a nine-hour explosion of earth and cinders, a massive cloud of smoke and ash rising 80,000 feet into the air and dumping ash across 11 states and parts of Canada.

We lived 300 miles from the volcano in the Spokane Valley.

That afternoon, I remember being on my bike and seeing a massive black cloud approaching, like the end of the world. I remember Mom yelling, "Get in the house." Then all went dark, and ash began raining down. It fell like a dusty, gray snow over everything. Ash clogged the sewers and choked car engines and closed the airport. We didn't know if it was toxic, so we had to stay inside for a couple of weeks and wear masks whenever we went out. We were trapped – everything canceled, schools, businesses, sports.

Of course, I think about this now, in the spring of 2020, as my family shelters in place because of the coronavirus pandemic. My daughters are already sick of each other. They are 16, 13 and 10, not far from the ages of Tanya, Patrick and me when the volcano erupted.

"Look," I tell the girls, "good things can come out of something like this. Maybe you three will grow closer."

They stare at me like I'm insane.

I tell them how their Uncle Patrick and I bonded back in 1980 over the volcano, how we gathered up ash and stored it in old Coke bottles and chewing tobacco tins. How we had plans to sell it to tourists.

I tell them how, the night of the eruption, I invited Patrick to sleep in my room because he was so scared. I tell them how we got bunk beds and shared a room for two years, until his mother got well enough to take him back.

"Wait, what?" the 16-year-old says.

Patrick lives with his wife and his son in Nevada now. He works at an auto body shop. My kids met him on our drive to Disneyland two years ago. I realize by the looks they're giving me now that they didn't know the family history. They just know him as Uncle Patrick.

"Uncle Patrick had a different mother?" the 13-year-old asks.

"That's not the point," I say. "What I'm saying is that you never know what will pull people together."

"Let's go back to Grampa's baby mama," the 16-year-old says. "No offense to your dirt collection, but I'd rather hear about that."

So, I tell them everything. Even the shoes.

It only lasted a day, my supervillain period. Patrick's teacher called my mom, and when I got home from school, she was waiting, seething, red-faced. She grabbed me by the arm and dragged me outside.

"What?" I said.

"Don't speak," she said.

She climbed in her car, a green AMC Gremlin. I got in the passenger side, indignant, arms crossed.

"What," I said again.

"Be quiet," she said. She was barely keeping it together. She drove us downtown, silent the whole way, and finally parked across from a brick apartment building.

"That's where Patrick and his mom lived," she said, "on the third floor. They had one room and a shared bathroom down the hall. Patrick's mother suffers from depression and had stopped sending Patrick to school. Then he got caught shoplifting potato chips from that store." She pointed to a newsstand across the street, P.M. Jacoy's. "When the police brought him home, they found him living in squalor, his mom catatonic on the couch. He'd been taking care of her."

I felt the first stirrings of deep shame, rumbling my core like an earthquake.

That's when Mom's calm melted away, and she grabbed my arm. "I am not going to let this turn you into an asshole, Tony!"

Tears spilled over her cheeks. "Listen. In your life, there will be disappointments, struggles, regrets. People will let you down. Make you angry. They will not live the way you want them to. And you have a choice. Live with empathy, or live with resentment. That's it!

"But know this: If you choose resentment, you will break my heart! Do you understand me?"

I did. Instantly. I could see it in her face. Empathy. Feeling for other people.

I imagined being the kind of person who would take in the kid your husband had with some other woman. How hard that must be. And yet she did it – without complaint or congratulations. She did it because it was right.

My shame erupted, and I began crying, too. I sat with Mom in that little green Gremlin, and we wept together. "OK," she said, finally. Then she squeezed my arm, started the car and drove us home. And somehow, she still had dinner on the table at 6.

 Jess Walter is the author of the *New York Times* bestselling novel *Beautiful Ruins*, *The Zero*, a finalist for the National Book Award, *Citizen Vince*, which won the Edgar Allan Poe Award; and three other novels. His story collection *We Live in Water* was released in 2013. His newest novel from Harper Perennial is *The Cold Millions*. A former reporter for *The Spokesman-Review*, Walter lives in Spokane with his family.

Acknowledgments

I would like to thank the two editors at *The Spokesman-Review* who have supported the Summer Stories project, retired editor Gary Graham and current editor Rob Curley. They have graciously allowed me to hog much of the Sunday Today section during the summer for seven years, and for that, fiction fans are grateful. Thanks to features editor Don Chareunsy for not chaffing at giving up valuable section front real estate for 17 weeks in 2020. I also have a special shout out to deputy features editor Kimberly Lusk, who has been my second set of eyes on every story since the beginning. Also deserving massive accolades is our staff artist Molly Quinn, who spends her summers meticulously crafting beautiful artworks to accompany these stories. Russel Davis with Gray Dog Press in Spokane offered his expertise and patience in helping us get this book just right.

And finally, I say thank you thank you thank you to all the authors over the years who have said yes to my request. It's been a joy to bring your creativity and your talents to *The Spokesman-Review*.

—Carolyn Lamberson